LITTLE BIG LEAGUE

LITTLE BIG LEAGUE

by Ronald Kidd

Based on the Castle Rock Entertainment
Motion Picture

Screenplay by Gregory K. Pincus
and Adam Scheinman

Story by Gregory K. Pincus

Turner Publishing, Inc.

ATLANTA

Published by Turner Publishing, Inc.
A Subsidiary of Turner Broadcasting System, Inc.
1050 Techwood Drive, N.W.
Atlanta, Georgia 30318

Distributed by Andrews and McMeel
A Universal Press Syndicate Company
4900 Main Street
Kansas City, Missouri 64112

ISBN 1-57036-135-5
First Edition 10 9 8 7 6 5 4 3 2 1

Printed in the U.S.A.

To
Paul Loscutoff,
who's going to hit a lot more homers before
his season's over
and
Yvonne Martin,
Minnesota Twins fan and grandmother extraordinaire

LITTLE BIG LEAGUE

1

Billy Heywood knew baseball.

Name a year, and he could tell you who won the batting title. Name a player, and he'd give you a quick rundown of strengths and weaknesses. He went to bed with the official rule book and woke up to the morning sports page. At age eleven, he was a walking baseball encyclopedia.

So why couldn't he hit?

Billy was wondering about this and other mysteries of life as he stood on deck one Saturday in late May. It was a perfect day for baseball in Minneapolis, the kind of day that makes you want to bottle the sunshine and save it for winter. And the day was about to get better because Billy's Little League team, down by two runs in the bottom of the ninth inning, had the bases loaded with nobody out.

Billy's mother and grandfather looked on from the stands.

"Come on, Billy," yelled Jenny Heywood. "Knock it out of the park!"

Thomas Heywood chuckled. "Relax, Jenny. He isn't up yet."

On the field, Billy called to his teammate Larry, who stood at the plate.

"Okay, Larry, be a hitter. Make sure it's your pitch, and keep your head in there."

The pitcher delivered and Larry swung. It was a long fly ball to deep left field. As the outfielder raced toward the fence, the runners paused, not sure whether the ball would be caught. The fielder lunged, but the ball hit the grass just beyond the reach of his glove.

"Go, Freddy, go, go!" Billy shouted to the runner on third.

Freddy scampered home easily. But the trip wasn't quite so easy for Sam, the runner on second. As he rounded third and started for home, he saw that the ball had beaten him there. He slammed on the brakes and headed back to third base.

Meanwhile Tommy, who had been on first, had raced around second and was standing on third, congratulating himself on his baserunning skills. And Larry, determined to stretch his hit into a triple, was pedaling toward third with his head down.

The catcher fired the ball to the third baseman, who bobbled it. As the ball hit the ground, Sam came sliding in from one direction and Larry from the other, both narrowly avoiding Tommy.

When the dust cleared, all three boys were standing on third base.

The third baseman did the only thing he could think of. He tagged them all.

Sam looked at Larry. Larry looked at Tommy. Tommy looked at Sam. Then everybody looked at the umpire.

"You're out!" he shouted.

"Who's out?" asked Sam.

The umpire shrugged. "Everybody, I guess."

Billy's manager, Mr. Lesnick, came racing out onto the field.

"Are you nuts?" he screamed at the umpire. "They're all safe!"

"What!" yelled the manager of the opposing team. "How can they be safe?"

Mr. Lesnick said, "They're all on the base, aren't they?"

"So what are you saying?" said the other manager. "They all just stand there? Then if the next guy gets a hit, all three of them run in?"

"Well, yeah. I think. Right, ump?"

They turned to the umpire, who had taken off his cap and was scratching his head. After a long silence, the umpire turned to Billy.

"Uh, Billy," said the umpire, "what's the call?"

Billy glanced apologetically at Mr. Lesnick. "Actually, the lead runner has possession of the bag. Sam's safe. Larry and Tommy are out."

"Are you sure?" asked the umpire.

"Yeah," Billy replied, "the same thing happened to the Brooklyn Dodgers back in 1926. Babe Hermann was the batter, and they ended up giving the base to Dazzy Vance."

"You heard the man," said the umpire. "Play ball!"

In the stands, Jenny Heywood turned to Thomas and asked, "What happened?"

"Billy told them. Lead runner gets the bag."

"Well, okay," said Jenny. "That sounds fair. Can I say it now?"

"Go ahead."

"Come on, Billy," she yelled. "Knock it out of the park!"

Billy stepped to the plate. There were two outs. The tying run was at third base. On the bench, Billy's friend Joey shouted encouragement. He was a freckle-faced boy with an easy grin.

"You heard your mom," he called. "Park one, Billy. Take him downtown."

"You know he's not going to hit a homer," said Billy's friend Chuck, who sat next to Joey. "Every time he tries, he swings too hard and misses."

"Oh yeah, right," Joey said. He yelled, "Forget the homer, Billy. How about getting hit by a pitch?"

Billy dug in, and the pitcher delivered. Billy closed his eyes and swung. He hit the ball! As it dribbled toward second, he lowered his head and ran as fast as he could down the first base line. Just before he reached the bag, he heard the smack of ball hitting glove.

The umpire punched the air. "You're out!"

Billy hung his head. He'd made the final out. The game was over.

Joey and Chuck brought him his mitt, and together they walked off the field.

"I should have worked the count," Billy said. "I can't believe I swung at the first pitch."

Chuck said, "I can't believe you actually hit the ball. Your eyes were closed."

"My eyes weren't closed. Tell him, Joey."

Joey closed his eyes and pretended to swing, stumbling to the ground. He lay there giggling.

"Great," said Billy. "Thanks a lot."

The boys reached the stands and found Jenny and Thomas Heywood waiting for them.

"Hi, Mom," Billy mumbled. "Hi, Grandpa."

"Billy, all you lost was a game," said his grandfather. "It's not the end of the world. It may take a little time, but you'll get over it."

Jenny added, "If you guys aren't too depressed, I was thinking we could go get some ice cream."

The boys looked at each other and took off, sprinting for the car.

Thomas Heywood watched them, smiling. "I think they just got over it."

Later, at the ice cream parlor, the boys waited at a table while Jenny and Thomas got the ice cream.

"It's so weird," said Chuck. "Your grandfather's like the richest man in the world, and nobody here even knows. They all think he's a normal person."

"He is," Billy said.

"You think he's richer than Mr. Howell?" asked Chuck. "You know, Thurston Howell III on *Gilligan's Island?*"

"I don't know. Maybe."

"What do you mean, maybe? He's got to be. Billy, your grandfather owns the Minnesota Twins. There's no way Mr. Howell has that much money."

"How do you know?" Joey asked.

"Think about it. If Mr. Howell was all that rich, what was he doing taking a cruise on the *S.S. Minnow?*"

Joey nodded. "Good point."

Jenny and Thomas returned to the table, sundaes in hand.

"Remember, boys," said Thomas, "eat as many of these as you can for the next fifteen years, because after that, you can't eat anything that tastes good for the rest of your life."

"Thanks, Mr. H.," said Chuck.

"Yeah," Joey said. "Good tip."

As the boys dug in, Thomas said, "You fellas want to come to the game tonight? We're playing the Angels."

Joey shook his head sadly. "I can't. I have to go to my grandmother's."

"I'm grounded," Chuck said.

Billy looked at him. "The egg incident?"

"Yeah," said Chuck.

"Now, boys," Thomas said, "I hope you're not just making up excuses because the Twins are losing."

Joey said, "No way, Mr. H. I'd rather see the worst team in history than go to my grandmother's house."

"Well, just remember, it's only May. A lot can happen."

The boys didn't know it, but Thomas Heywood was right. This summer, the Minnesota Twins would have one of the most unusual seasons in the history of baseball. And Billy would be right in the middle of it.

2

It was a chilly forty-two degrees in Minneapolis, but that didn't bother the Minnesota Twins. They played their home games in the Metrodome, a covered stadium where the temperature at game time was always a comfortable seventy-two degrees.

It was even more comfortable in the owner's box where Billy and his grandfather lounged in plush chairs, watching the Twins play the California Angels.

The crowd roared as Lou Collins drove a clean single to left field. Billy grinned at his grandfather.

"Boy, Grandpa, it was a great move signing Lou to a multi-year deal."

"You think so, huh?"

"Yeah," said Billy. "I just wish O'Farrell would use him better. He hits him behind Kain, so nobody's protecting him in the order. And why does he keep batting Hilbert eighth? He's got the second highest on-base percentage on the team."

As they spoke, Arthur Goslin, the Twins' general manager, approached from behind them.

"Another George O'Farrell fan, huh?" he said.

"Now, Arthur," Thomas Heywood replied, "don't start in again. You're my general manager. You're supposed to back me."

"Hi, Mr. Goslin," said Billy.

Thomas continued, "You may not like O'Farrell's personality, but—"

"I know, I know," Arthur said. "He's a good baseball man."

"Arthur, I'm convinced we have the talent to win. Something's been missing. I just can't put my finger on it. I'm hoping a little jolt from a guy like O'Farrell might make the difference."

In this game, as it turned out, the only jolt was a grand-slam home run by the Angels. Afterward, a dejected group of players filed into the Twins' locker room. There they found manager George O'Farrell in a shouting match with his pitching coach, Mac McNally.

"Listen, Mac," O'Farrell bellowed, "I don't have to answer to you. I'm the manager. Case closed. You don't like the way I handle the pitchers, feel free to leave."

"Fine," grunted McNally, and he stormed out of the room.

O'Farrell shouted after him, "There are plenty of pitching coaches out there. Plenty of them. And you know what? Some of them can actually fit into their uniforms."

Rookie shortstop Mickey Scales suppressed a giggle, and O'Farrell whirled around.

"Scales, you think that's funny? I'll tell you what's funny. It's that thing you call a swing. You'd better start hitting, pal, or you're heading back to Triple A. And that goes for the rest of you clowns. You're a sorry excuse for a ball club."

O'Farrell stormed into his office, almost running over relief pitcher and resident cutup Jim Bowers. Bowers just shook his head, a goofy smile on his face. As he did, Billy and Thomas Heywood entered the locker room.

"Tough game, fellas," said Thomas. "We'll get them next time."

As usual, Billy drifted over to Lou Collins's locker.

"How you doing, Billy?" said Lou. "You staying out of trouble?"

"Sure."

"Yeah? Well, don't let me hear different. How's your mom?"

"Good," Billy said. "She's kind of busy, but she's doing good."

"She's a nice lady. Be sure and say hi for me, will you?"

"Okay."

Jerry Johnson, an aging veteran and another one of Billy's favorites, strolled by.

"Billy, how'd you do today?"

"Hey, Jerry. Not so great. I grounded out to end the game."

"Did you do what I told you?" Jerry asked. "Did you keep your weight back and your shoulder in?"

"Yeah, I did everything, but I still can't hit. I think the problem is I'm a spazmo."

Jerry ruffled Billy's hair. "Nah, come on. It just takes practice. We'll work on it some more. You'll get it."

Just then, the door to the manager's office opened and O'Farrell stepped out.

"Hey, who let that kid in here?" he snarled.

"I did, George," said Thomas.

"Oh, it's Billy. Sorry, Mr. H. My mistake."

Thomas smiled thinly. "That's all right, George. We all make mistakes. That's why we have dry cleaners."

On the way home that night, Billy's grandfather was quiet. Finally he said, "You know, Billy, a game like tonight really puts me in a bad mood. Guess I'm just going to have to take it out on you."

"Take your best shot, Grandpa."

"All right, 1951, Dodgers and Giants. Ralph Branca was on the mound—"

"That's too easy," Billy interrupted. "Bobby Thomson hit a home run and the Giants won the pennant."

"Yes, he did. But here's my question. Who was on deck?"

"On deck?"

"That's the question."

"Jeez," said Billy. "I have no idea."

"It was a young man named Willie Mays."

Billy stared at him. "No way."

"Way," said his grandfather.

When they pulled up to Billy's house, Thomas Heywood was still chuckling. He put his arm around Billy's shoulders and walked him to the door.

"Okay, here's an easy one," said Billy. "Who was the first black player ever to play in the major leagues?"

"You'd like me to say Jackie Robinson, but I'm not going to. Fleet Walker, Toledo. I believe it was 1884."

"Boy, you really are in a bad mood."

Inside, Billy's mom pecked Thomas on the cheek and gave Billy a big hug.

"How was it?" she asked.

"We lost," Billy said. "But it was still fun."

"Great. Now, into your room and ready for bed."

"Okay," he replied. "Thanks, Grandpa."

"Anytime, son."

Billy headed down the hallway, then stopped.

"Oh, yeah, I forgot," he told his mother. "Lou said hi again."

As Billy ducked into his room, Thomas Heywood turned to his daughter-in-law.

"He's an awful nice young fella, that Lou."

"Thomas—"

"Look, Jenny, I know you loved my son. But I think it would be good for Billy to have a man around the house. And I'm sure you could think of a couple of things to do with one yourself."

"Thomas!"

"That's all right, I'm old. I'm allowed to say whatever I want." Chuckling, he opened the door to leave.

"Oh, I almost forgot," he said. "Is it okay for Billy to go to the game on Tuesday? It's Boston. Roger Clemens is pitching."

"Oh, no, you don't," Jenny said. "Not on a school night."

"Jenny, it's Roger Clemens, the greatest strikeout pitcher in the game. Billy's never seen him in person."

"I can't help that."

"You know," said Thomas, "when I was Billy's age, I had a chance to see Walter Johnson pitch. The Big Train, they called him. But I didn't go. I can't even remember why. Maybe I thought I'd see him another time, but I didn't."

Thomas shook his head. "He was an all-time great, and I never saw him play. When you get to be my age, you realize you only get one shot at this thing, and it doesn't last forever. So when you get a chance to see something really special, you don't pass it up."

Jenny sighed and shook her head, smiling. "Well, if you're going to resort to wisdom, I guess I don't have much choice. I'll tell you what. Billy has a science project due on Tuesday. If he gets it done, he can go. But don't bet on it. He's not exactly the world's most diligent student."

"I have faith in him," Thomas said.

Around the corner and out of sight, Billy grinned and pumped his fist. "Yesss!"

3

"Rocket Roger Clemens!" said Chuck. "How'd you pull this one off?" Billy shrugged. "I got my science project done, didn't I? That was the deal."

It was Tuesday and school had just let out. Billy, Chuck, and Joey were in science class, taking one last look at Billy's science project before heading home. The project was a model of a volcano, complete with gray puffs of cotton billowing out the top and melted orange crayons flowing down the sides.

Chuck said in a low voice, "Of course you got it done. It's the same volcano you turned in last year to Mrs. Dugar."

"This is way different," said Billy. "Last year was Mount Vesuvius. This is Mount St. Helens. See, I added all these trees."

"Oh, yeah," Joey said, "I didn't even see that." He pointed to a green toothpick with little pieces of grass pasted on the sides. "Is that a spruce?"

Billy gathered up his books and said, "Gentlemen, I'd love to stay and chat, but the Rocket calls."

He nodded to his friends, slipped out the classroom door, and took off running down the hall.

"Heywood!" called a voice behind him.

Screeching to a halt, Billy turned and faced Mr. Patterson, the school principal. Billy offered a weak smile.

"Uh, hi, Mr. Patterson," he said.

"Young man," Mr. Patterson answered, glowering at him, "this is the third time I've had to warn you about running in the halls. Perhaps a little time in my office might slow you down."

Billy glanced at his watch. His grandfather was due to pick him up in just a half hour. "Please, Mr. Patterson, not today. I promise, it won't happen again."

The principal eyed Billy skeptically, tapping his foot on the hallway floor. It sounded like the pounding of a judge's gavel. Finally, Mr. Patterson sighed and shook his head.

"Well," he said, "see that it doesn't happen again."

"Thanks, sir. It won't."

Mr. Patterson turned and walked away. As soon as he was around the corner and out of sight, Billy took off running again. Bursting out the door and into the sunshine, he leaped onto his bike and sped off down the road.

He was on his way to see Roger Clemens!

Ten minutes later, Billy skidded around the corner onto his street. Hopping the curb in front of his house, he stored the bike in the garage and pushed open the front door.

"Mom, I'm home!" he called. "Listen, you don't have to make me anything for dinner. I'll get a couple of dogs at the game."

He hurried into his room, dropped his books on the bed, and looked in the closet for his mitt. It wasn't there. He checked the rest of the room and found baseball cards, posters, bats, pennants, and enough autographed balls to open a small museum. But no mitt.

He headed for the kitchen, calling, "Mom, what did you do with my mitt? I can't find it anywhere."

When he entered the kitchen, he stopped. His mother was sitting at the table, her eyes red and puffy from crying.

"Mom?"

Jenny Heywood looked up, her lip quivering. Billy thought she had the saddest face he had ever seen.

"Billy," she said. "It's Grandpa."

❖ ❖ ❖

The funeral was held three days later. Billy and his mother were there, along with Thomas Heywood's many friends and associates, including the entire Minnesota Twins team. There was a brief service at the grave, where Lou Collins spoke for the rest of the players.

"Even though he was an owner," Lou said, "you never felt like he owned *you*. He listened to you. He respected you. And he found the good in you, which wasn't always so easy with this bunch. He signed me when I was seventeen years old, and ever since, he's been my boss. But through all the years, I've only thought of him one way: Thomas Heywood was my friend."

Lou glanced around the graveside. His eyes came to rest on Jenny, who was dabbing her eyes with a handkerchief. As he gazed at her, he said, "The world just lost a real good guy."

"Mom," Billy asked in a voice that trembled and broke, "why did *he* have to die? Why couldn't somebody bad die?"

Then he buried his face in her dress and cried.

4

When looking for a lawyer, most people as wealthy as Thomas Heywood would have headed downtown to one of the powerful law firms with high-rise offices and rates to match. But in this respect, as in many others, he was an unusual man.

His choice was a smaller firm, housed in a modest building on the edge of town, with people he liked and trusted. The lawyer he trusted the most was Margaret Sullivan. It was she who had helped Thomas draw up his will, and it was she who showed the document to Jenny and Billy in her office a few days after the funeral.

Margaret Sullivan explained the contents of the written will, then leaned back in her desk chair.

"Now, Jennifer," she said, "after your husband, Thomas, Jr., passed away, your father-in-law videotaped a personal message as an addition to his will. I've got it here."

She reached into her desk, removed a tape, and loaded it into the VCR. There was static, then a basketball game.

"And so," the announcer was saying, "the Bulls' lead is cut to two, with just under six minutes to play."

"The message is coming up," Margaret said. "He taped it over a game."

Jenny couldn't help smiling. That was Thomas, all right.

And suddenly, there he was, grinning at them from the screen. Billy stared. It was as if his grandfather had come back to life.

"Hi, Jenny, Billy," he said. "Well, if you're watching this tape, I guess I'm dead. I'm sorry. Still, I had a pretty good run, huh?"

Jenny nodded and dabbed at her eyes.

Thomas went on, "And, hey, for all I know, Billy, you may be forty-eight years old by now. I hope so, because that means I lived to be a hundred and seven. It also means we got to spend a lot of time together."

Jenny reached over and took her son's hand. She wished she could take her father-in-law's hand, too.

"Anyway," Thomas was saying, "Margaret, my lawyer, assuming *she's* still alive, will fill you in on all the details of my will. But the reason I made this tape is that there's one item I wanted to tell you about myself. Billy, you're my best friend in the world. And so I'd like you to have my very favorite thing—the Minnesota Twins."

All of a sudden, Billy could hear the pounding of his heart. Over that sound, Thomas Heywood kept talking.

"Now, it's possible you may still be a little young. If that's the case, Arthur and all the people in the organization can run the day-to-day business for you. Let them do their jobs. But remember, Billy, I'm doing this because I have faith in you. You love baseball, and you know more about the game than anyone I've ever known. I don't care how young you may be, Billy. I trust you."

Thomas gazed out at Billy, then blew him a kiss.

"Take care of your mother," he said. "She's the best."

And then he was gone.

Two basketball players went up for a rebound. "—and that's twelve boards for Smith tonight, eight in this half!" the announcer was saying.

Margaret Sullivan clicked off the TV and turned to Billy. "Isn't that wonderful? Your grandfather gave you the Twins."

Billy got up from his chair, walked to the window, and looked outside. After what seemed like a very long time, he turned back to the lawyer.

"I'd rather have my grandfather," he said.

❖ ❖ ❖

"So let me get this straight," Joey said the next day as he and Chuck walked Billy home from school. "You own the team *and* the stadium?"

"Uh-huh."

"That's unbelievable. Can I borrow five bucks?"

Before Billy could answer, an attractive older girl approached.

"Um, you're like, Billy Heywood, right?" she said.

"Well, yeah," he replied.

She took a pen from her notebook and held it toward him. "Um, could I, like, have your autograph?"

"Huh? My autograph?"

"Could you, like, make it out to Shelly?" she said.

Billy shrugged and said, "Uh, sure."

He signed her notebook and handed the pen back. The girl smiled shyly.

"I can't believe it. Thanks."

As she walked off, Joey stared. "Wow. Shelly Hogeboom. What a babe."

"Well, Billy," said Chuck, shaking his head admiringly, "let's see you top that one."

Billy thought for a minute, then grinned. "You're on," he said.

An hour later, they were standing on the deserted infield of the Metrodome.

"So, what do you think?" Billy asked his friends.

"It's a lot better than Shelly Hogeboom," Joey said.

Chuck ran over to the third-base dugout and picked up a baseball.

"Hey, Joey, get on first," he called. "Let me see if I can make the throw from third."

Joey trotted to the bag, and Chuck went into his best imitation of Wally Holland, the Twins' announcer. He intoned, "Lou Collins, normally a first baseman, is down at third today. And, oh, he makes a great stop, and here's the throw to first—"

Chuck lofted the ball across the diamond. It hit the pitcher's mound and rolled to a stop on the artificial turf.

"Good arm, Lou," Joey giggled.

As the boys laughed, a security guard hurried out onto the field.

"Hey, what are you kids doing? How'd you get in here, anyway?"

"You don't understand," said Chuck. "He's Billy Heywood."

"Is that supposed to mean something to me?" the guard asked.

Billy said, "Mr. Goslin can tell you who I am."

"He can? Could I see some I.D.?"

"I.D.?" Billy asked. "I'm eleven. What kind of I.D. would I have?"

The guard jerked his thumb toward the exit. "All right, come on, guys. Out! You're going to get me in trouble."

Just then, Arthur Goslin stuck his head out of the dugout. When he saw what was happening, he strode out onto the field.

"No, no, no," Arthur told the guard. "Roberts, this is Billy Heywood. He owns the ball club."

"He does?" said Roberts, looking back and forth from Billy to Arthur and then back again.

"Yes," Arthur replied, "I assure you he does."

"He's short for his age," Joey explained.

Embarrassed, Roberts removed his cap and turned to Billy.

"I'm really sorry, Mr. Heywood. It's my first week on the job. I just didn't know."

"No problem," said Billy. "Listen, I need to talk to Mr. Goslin. Is it okay if my friends hang out and throw the ball around a little?"

Roberts said, "Sure thing, Mr. Heywood. You got it. I'll make sure they're not disturbed."

"Thanks."

Billy nodded to his friends and followed Arthur into the dugout. On the field, Chuck looked around the vast expanse of the Metrodome.

"How great is this?" he murmured. Then he picked up the ball and threw it to Joey at first.

The stands were empty, and the stadium was silent.

5

The next day, Billy continued his conversation at the Metrodome with Arthur Goslin. The stands were still empty, but this time the field was a beehive of activity because the Minnesota Twins were working out.

In right field, players stretched and ran wind sprints. In left, outfielders practiced catching fly balls and throwing to home plate. Infielders stood two-deep at their positions, taking turns fielding ground balls.

Billy and Arthur sat in the first row of the stands, talking quietly and watching the players. As they spoke, they noticed a pitcher practicing his curve ball on the sidelines. He wore a three-day beard, a thick Fu Manchu mustache, and a uniform that revealed a bulging chest and legs like tree trunks. He was the Twins' ace relief pitcher, John "Blackout" Gatling.

Billy and Arthur weren't the only ones who had spotted him. Manager George O'Farrell approached and lit into him.

"Blackout, we didn't trade for you because of your curve ball. I don't like your curve ball. In fact, I hate your curve ball. You want to know why? Because it doesn't curve, that's why. Let me make this simple for you, you cement head. Wait for the guy behind the plate to stick one finger down, then throw the ball as hard as you can. Got it?"

Billy watched O'Farrell stomp off, then he hopped over the railing and said to Blackout, "Hi, I'm Billy Heywood. I think you've got a great curve ball. You're just dropping down a little on the release."

Blackout's bushy eyebrows shot up like a pair of startled caterpillars. But before he could say anything, Billy had trotted off in O'Farrell's direction. Billy caught up with the manager by the water cooler.

"Mr. O'Farrell?" he said. "You know, I've been thinking, you really scream a lot at the guys. Maybe it's not such a good thing."

"Oh, really," said O'Farrell, looking up from the cooler. "You think I yell too much."

"Yeah, it's like in school. I could do good in math, except Mr. Smid's always yelling at me. And when he yells, I get nervous. I've lost total confidence in my long division."

O'Farrell rolled his eyes. "Long division. You don't say. Look, kid, your grandfather wanted someone to rattle their cages, and that's just what I'm doing. Got it?"

"I know that. But it isn't working. So . . . could you just stop? Please?"

O'Farrell crossed his arms and gazed down at Billy. Then he sighed. "Yeah, sure, kid."

He took a gulp of water, then headed back out onto the field. On the way, he spotted something.

"Hamilton!" he screamed. "Hey, Hamilton, you idiot!"

At the end of practice, Billy's mother arrived to pick him up. On her way across the field she passed Lou Collins.

"Hi," she said, smiling.

Lou returned the smile. "So, how does it feel to have a major league owner for a son?"

"It's a little strange. But we have an understanding. Billy may be the owner, but I'm still the boss."

"Sounds fair," he chuckled.

"Anyway, I was just looking for him. You know where he is?"

"In the clubhouse, I think."

"Thanks," she said. "Well, see you later, I guess."

As Jenny moved away, Lou said, "Uh, wait a sec. I was just wondering . . . does Billy have a birthday coming up?"

"Yes, the twenty-second. How did you know?"

Lou blushed. "Well, uh . . . I got invited."

"To Valley Fair?"

"Yeah."

Jenny asked, "How many of Billy's other new friends did he invite?"

"Just Jerry, but he can't make it. Well . . . are you going to be there?"

"Of course," she said. "You think I'd miss my chance to ride the Thundering Frog?"

He laughed. "I guess not. So, would you mind if I went? I mean, it wouldn't look good, me snubbing an invite to the boss's big party."

"I think you're right," she said, smiling. "That wouldn't look good at all."

A few days later, between classes at school, Billy, Chuck, and Joey stood at their lockers.

"So what do you think?" Chuck was saying. "Tonight? The mall?"

Billy shook his head. "I can't. I've got too much homework."

"Homework? You own the Twins!"

"Yeah," Joey chimed in, "if I owned the Twins I wouldn't even show up here. I'd just hire a whole bunch of scientists to do my homework. I mean, if you're rich, you don't have to be smart. This is America."

As he finished, a voice thundered through the hall. "Heywood!"

It was Mr. Patterson.

Billy said, "Mr. Patterson, I wasn't running. I wasn't even walking."

"Would you please come to my office?" he said.

Chuck and Joey looked at each other, then began edging away.

"I, uh, guess we'd better be getting to class," Joey said.

"So long, Billy," said Chuck. "It's been nice knowing you."

They took off down the hall—not running, but walking very fast. When they were gone, Mr. Patterson turned on his heel and said, "Follow me, Heywood."

He led Billy into his office, where he pushed a button on his phone and held out the receiver toward Billy.

"It's for you," he said.

Billy stared dumbly at the phone, then took it and said, "Hello?"

"Big news," said Arthur at the other end. "The commissioner's office just declared Rickey Henderson a free agent."

"Wow," Billy said. "Rickey Henderson."

"The Jays breached his contract," Arthur went on. "And here's the best part: his people contacted us. We've got a shot at him."

"That's great!"

Mr. Patterson, meanwhile, was beside himself with excitement. "What is it?" he asked, leaning forward in his chair. "Is it a trade? A big trade?"

Billy covered the phone with his hand. "Sorry, Mr. Patterson. I can't talk about it. I'm sure you understand."

Later, after school, Billy walked to the bike rack with Chuck and Joey.

"So here it is," he told them. "Rickey wants a three-year deal. Eighteen million. He wants a house, a golf membership at Fair Oaks, a dog, and a Ferrari Testarosa."

"He wants a dog?" Joey said.

Billy shrugged. "An albino Russian wolfhound. That's what he wants."

"You've got to give it to him," said Chuck. "It's Rickey Henderson."

"Yeah," Joey added, "you've got to. Give him two dogs."

Billy said, "O'Farrell thinks he's a bad influence. He said if we try and sign Henderson, he'll quit."

"Who cares?" said Chuck. "O'Farrell's a jerk."

"Yeah, well, still, I've got to think about it."

Billy was still thinking about it that night as he watched the Twins on TV while doing his homework.

"Hey," said his mother when she walked into the room, "I thought I told you about studying with the TV on."

"I'm just recopying. Honest."

He showed her his paper, and she read the title. "'Ben Franklin, M.V.P. of the Continental Congress'? Finish it up tomorrow, huh? It's a school night, and it's way past your bedtime."

"Mom, I think you're really too caught up in this whole 'school night' thing."

"Billy," she said, pointing. "Bed."

He sighed. "I bet the other owners get to stay up and watch their teams."

"The other owners don't have math first period."

Billy clicked off the TV set, closed his books, and climbed under the covers.

"It stinks being a kid," he said.

His mother tucked him in and gave him a peck on the cheek. "Good night, honey. I love you."

"I love you, too, Mom. Good night."

She turned out the lights and closed the door behind her. As soon as she was gone, Billy reached under his pillow and pulled out a radio. He put on the earphones, turned up the volume, and smiled as he watched the Twins play ball on the inside of his eyelids.

6

"He's a great ballplayer!" said Arthur Goslin.

George O'Farrell shook his head. "I don't want him. I had a run-in with him when I was third base coach with the Yankees."

"You had a run-in with everybody when you were third base coach with the Yankees."

"I don't want him!" yelled O'Farrell.

It was late the following afternoon, and the Rickey Henderson issue still had not been settled. Goslin and O'Farrell were thrashing it out in the manager's office, as Billy looked on quietly. Finally he spoke up.

"Mr. O'Farrell, with all due respect, you're acting like a first grader."

"All right, that's it!" fumed O'Farrell. "I've put up with this long enough. You want to play with your little buddies up in the owner's box, that's fine. Just stay out of my office, out of my clubhouse, and off of my field. Got it?"

"Yes, sir."

"Good," said O'Farrell. "So why don't you go home and build a fort or something?"

"I think I have a better idea," Billy said.

Later, tossing horseshoes in the backyard, Billy told Chuck and Joey about the confrontation.

"It was really weird," he said. "I never fired anyone before. And the funny thing is, it didn't even matter. Henderson re-signed with Toronto."

"So who are you getting to replace O'Farrell?" Chuck asked.

"I don't know. Whitey Herzog turned us down. Same with Valentine. None of the good guys want to work for a kid."

Chuck said, "You should do it yourself."

"Yeah, right. Get real."

"You get real," said Chuck. "You'd be great."

Billy stopped in the middle of a horseshoe toss and turned to Chuck. "Do you know how hard it is to manage?"

"It's the American League. They use designated hitters. How hard can it be?"

Joey said, "Think of it. You could lead the Twins to the pennant. Become Manager of the Year. Billy, man, the Twins need you."

Billy stared at Joey, then back at Chuck. They were serious. And suddenly, so was he.

"You what!" croaked Arthur Goslin.

"You heard me," said Billy. "I'm going to manage the Twins."

Arthur rolled his eyes, then began pacing back and forth in his office while Mac McNally watched.

"Billy," said Arthur, "we'd be the laughing stock of baseball."

"Not if we win."

A tired smile creased Mac's weathered face. He said, "Come on, son. Be serious."

"I am serious. You'd help me, wouldn't you, Mac?"

"Billy, it's not that easy. There's a lot to this game. A lot. It's all situations. Situations and tendencies. And the more you've seen, the more you know what to do."

"Okay," said Billy, crossing his arms. "Try me. Make up a situation."

"All right," Mac said, "here's one. We're playing the Yankees. No one out. Scales at first, great speed. Lou's at bat, two balls and a strike. Abbott's on the mound. Lefty. Lonnie's on deck. And

33

remember, he's a switch hitter. What do you do?"

"What's the score?" Billy asked.

"Tie game."

"What inning? Home or away?"

"Eighth," Mac replied. "Home."

Billy said, "Who's catching? Who's rested in the bullpen? Who's up in the ninth for the Yanks?"

Mac glanced uneasily at Arthur. "Nokes," he answered. "Everybody. Seven, eight, nine."

"Nokes can't throw," Billy said, "but still I let Lou hit away. With Mattingly holding Scales, he's got that big hole to hit to."

"No," said Mac. "You've got lefty against lefty. You only need one run. Lou's a good bunter. You sacrifice the go-ahead run to second with only one out."

Billy shook his head. "If you sacrifice him to second, they walk Lonnie and bring in Steve Farr to pitch to Spencer. So you've taken the bat out of our two best hitters, our three and four men, and we've got Spencer, a righty with no speed, against Farr and his palm ball, which means . . ."

"Double play," Mac admitted. "But you could pinch hit for Spencer."

Billy said, "Now you've taken the bat out of our three, four, and five hitters. Not exactly a great trip through the heart of our order."

Arthur stared at Billy, then looked over at Mac and shrugged. "Any questions?"

"Yeah," said Mac. "What does he need me for?"

Arthur picked up the phone and dialed. A few moments later he had the commissioner of baseball on the line, and he was selling his heart out.

"Look, Commissioner," Arthur was saying, "the kid's for real. He knows this team inside and out. Yes, sir, I understand, but Mac

34

will stay on as pitching coach and . . ."

"Tell him about the attendance," Billy said.

". . . and to tell you the truth, sir, we could really use the publicity. We're dying here. It's only June, and people are already talking about football. Just imagine the fan interest. Huh? His mother?"

Arthur looked up at Billy, who thought for a second, then whispered something into Arthur's ear.

"Yes, sir," Arthur said, "his mother said it was okay with her if it was okay with you."

It was one of the most unusual press conferences ever held at the Metrodome. Dozens of reporters had been sent from all over the country to interview an eleven-year-old boy. Of course, this wasn't just any eleven-year-old boy. This was the new manager of the Minnesota Twins.

Jenny Heywood peered out at the reporters from behind a curtain.

"Are you sure the commissioner approved this?" she asked Billy.

"Absolutely. He said it was okay with him if it was okay with you."

"I don't know," she said. "The more I think about this . . ."

"Mom," Billy broke in, "you said you wanted me to do something constructive this summer. You said, 'Jimmy Brackman has a job. Why can't *you* get a job.'"

"Jimmy Brackman is a paper boy."

Billy threw up his hands. "Oh, you mean you just don't want me to get a *good* job."

"What about your friends?" she asked.

"It was their idea to begin with. They'd kill for this chance."

Still seeing doubt in her eyes, Billy took his mother's hand.

"Mom, trust me," he said. "Grandpa did."

35

She took a deep breath and squared her shoulders. Holding out her hand, she said, "Give me your gum."

Billy handed it to her. Then he pulled the curtain aside and walked out to face the reporters.

"There he is!" someone said.

Light bulbs flashed, and the room grew quiet. Billy looked out at the crowd.

"First of all," he said, "I'd just like to say that this is really cool. Now . . ."

He reached into his pocket and pulled out a sheet of notebook paper, then unfolded it and began reading.

"Hall of Famer Bob Lemon once said, 'Baseball was made for kids, and grown-ups only screw it up.' With this in mind, I would like to announce that I have named myself the new manager of the Minnesota Twins, effective as of tomorrow night, at which time my commitment to Theodore Jeffries Elementary School will be complete."

For a moment there was complete silence. Then the place went crazy. Arthur handed a Twins cap to Billy, who put it on and looked out over the room.

"Any questions?" he called above the racket. A dozen reporters leaped to their feet, jostling each other to get his attention.

Billy smiled. He decided he was going to like this job.

7

The night of Billy's debut, the players milled around the clubhouse before the game, doing what players always do: scratch, spit, and complain. Somehow outfielder Spencer Hamilton was managing to do all three at once.

"How do they expect us to play for a kid?" he asked. "How's he going to know strategy?"

Jerry Johnson snorted. "What do you care? You never throw to the right base anyway."

"Bite me," said Hamilton.

Tucker Kain shook his head, saying, "There's no way a kid can pull this off."

"I don't know, man," replied Lonnie Ritter, another outfielder. "Kids today are amazing. I played winter ball down in Venezuela. They had kids half his age, every one of them speaking Spanish. And that's a hard language."

Second baseman Pat Corning said, "I thought that slump in 1991 was the low point of my career. But this is worse."

"It's not cool, man. It's definitely not cool," piped up Larry Hilbert, the third baseman. He turned to Lou Collins. "What are you going to do, Lou?"

"Pretty much what I always do," Lou said as he laced his shoes. "If I'm in the lineup, I'll play. If I'm not, I won't."

Relief pitcher Jim Bowers sat nearby, his arm packed in ice. "Does anybody else find it disconcerting that our new manager can't get into an R-rated movie for another six years?"

The door opened and Billy walked in, wearing his Twins'

uniform for the first time. Everyone saw him but pitcher Mike McGrevey.

"Well, I don't know about the rest of you geniuses," said McGrevey, "but I'm not putting up with this. I'm a free agent next year. And I'm not going let my career be ruined by some mutant Little Leaguer."

The room grew quiet. Billy took a deep breath. Then, forcing a grin, he walked past McGrevey, saying, "Hi, guys."

There was no response. Billy moved over to Mark Hodges, the Twins' catcher.

"Hey, Mark," he said. "How's your knee?"

"Why, are you the trainer now, too?" Hodges asked.

"I was just trying to be friendly."

Hodges said, "You want a friend, get a dog."

Billy searched the room for a friendly face. He found it in Mac, who winked at him and nodded.

"Well," Billy said, "since it's already quiet, I guess we might as well start the pregame meeting."

He climbed up on a chair and looked around at the team. "I'm going to make this short, although I should practice, since I have public speaking next year."

McGrevey muttered, "This is going to be even worse than I thought."

"Anyway, here's what I want to say," Billy went on. "I think this team is great. Look who we got. We got Lou Collins and Lonnie Ritter. You guys are All-Stars. We've got speed, we've got defense, we've got pitching. We've got it all. We can win this thing!"

Sneering, Hamilton said, "Well, I'm psyched."

"Look," said Billy, "I know you think I'm a joke, and maybe I am. But I'll make you a deal. Just play hard for a couple of weeks. After that, if you don't like the way I'm managing, if we're not winning . . . then I'll fire myself."

He gazed right at Hamilton, who finally looked away.

Billy said, "I'm dedicating this season to my grandpa, so even if you don't want to do it for me, do it for him."

No one said a word. Lou looked on sympathetically as Billy climbed down from the chair and walked out of the clubhouse.

The game was just minutes away. In the bullpen, the starting pitchers were warming up. In the press box, Twins' announcer Wally Holland was doing the same.

He leaned into his microphone and sang out, "Hello, everybody! This is Wally Holland, welcoming you to the Metrodome for a historic event—eleven-year-old Billy Heywood's managerial debut. The atmosphere is electric, the sell-out crowd all here to see what the boy wonder can do."

At that moment, the boy wonder was in uniform on the field, searching the stands for his mother. He spotted her in the first row next to the dugout, sitting with Chuck and Joey. As he trotted over, a herd of reporters followed.

Jenny grinned. "Good luck, honey!"

"Thanks, Mom," he said. She hugged him, and a dozen flashbulbs went off.

"Look, Billy," said Chuck, "I don't want to make you nervous or anything, but Shelly Hogeboom is sitting in section 121."

Joey said, "Hey, do you have the lineup card?"

Billy nodded and handed him the card. Glancing over it, Joey said, "I can't believe you're not starting Wedman. He kills the Tigers."

Glancing toward home plate, Billy noticed the four umpires waiting for him, along with the Tiger manager.

"Look, I've got to go," he said, taking the card back.

"Not with that dirty face you won't," said Jenny. She wet her handkerchief and began dabbing at his cheeks.

39

"Mom," Billy moaned, "the guys are watching."

"Don't be silly. Nobody's looking."

In the outfield, the giant scoreboard showed a closeup of Jenny Heywood cleaning Billy's face. When she noticed the scoreboard, she turned a bright red, and the crowd cheered.

As Billy approached home plate, the cheers grew in volume, building into a wall of sound. Billy stopped, dazed, and looked up into the stands. He didn't know what would happen on the field tonight or for the rest of the summer. But for now, he was one happy kid.

8

The pregame activities had been fun, but there was still a baseball game to be played. The Twins took the field a few minutes later, hoping to end a season-long slump.

Manager Billy Heywood took his post on the top step of the dugout, where he watched his team turn in a solid performance for the first six innings.

In the bottom of the seventh, the Twins' Lonnie Ritter reached first on a single, and Mark Hodges stepped to the plate. Billy turned to Mac McNally.

"Let's hit and run," he said. Mac nodded and signaled the play.

When Hodges stepped back into the box, the Tigers' catcher said to him, "You boys going out for milk and cookies after the game?"

"Probably," Hodges snarled back.

As the pitcher wound up, Lonnie took off for second. Instead of swinging to protect the runner, Hodges let the pitch fly past him. Lonnie was easily thrown out.

In the dugout, Mac was fuming. "I can't believe it! Hodges missed the sign."

Billy said, "He didn't miss it."

"What are you talking about? He didn't even swing. He hung Lonnie out to dry."

"I know," said Billy.

As the game went on, it was turning out to be an important run. Going into the bottom of the ninth, the Twins were trailing by one. They made one quick out, and Pat Corning, a weak hitter, was due up.

Billy called down the bench, "Jerry, grab a bat."

Jerry Johnson, the former superstar who was struggling to hang on with the team, took a few practice swings and strode to the plate to pinch hit for Corning.

Mac shot Billy a questioning look, but Billy brushed it off. "He's a pro, Mac. He'll come through."

In the broadcast booth, Wally Holland had his doubts as well.

"Jerry Johnson, celebrating his eleventh season with the Twins, has had a rough go of it so far," said Holland. "Not many at-bats, his batting average one ninety-four, nearly eighty points below his career average. Last year, though, he was sixth in the American League at hitting lefthanders he was facing for the first time after the seventh inning. At home. So that's something to keep in mind."

The fans kept it in mind as Johnson hit a slow ground ball to third and was thrown out by twenty feet.

"So," Holland continued, "that leaves it up to twenty-year-old rookie shortstop Mickey Scales. He hasn't shown much with the stick this year, and I'm a little surprised young Billy is letting him hit.

"Scales steps in. He taps the plate with his bat. Looks a little nervous up there. All right, here's the windup, and the pitch. There's a lazy fly ball to left. This should do it. Phillips is under the ball . . . and this game is over."

In the clubhouse after the game, the press swarmed around Billy.

"Come on, give him some room," said Mac.

"Billy," called out one reporter, "let me have the honor of being the first person to second-guess you. If you could do it again, would you pinch hit for Scales in the ninth? After all, in the last four games—"

"Mickey's the one I wanted up there," Billy broke in. "We

needed an extra base hit, and he's got great power to the gaps. I wouldn't even think of pinch hitting for him."

Across the room, Scales turned to Jim Bowers. "Hey, I like this kid. He's all right."

"Of course you do," said Bowers. "He's the only guy in the world who thinks you can hit."

Another reporter spoke up. "Billy, what about that steal with Lonnie in the seventh? Still think that was the right call?"

Mac said, "That wasn't a steal. It was—"

"I made a mistake there," said Billy, cutting Mac off. "If I had it to do over again, I'd probably call for a hit and run."

Hearing the exchange, Hodges unlaced his shoes in silence.

Later, after the reporters and most of the team had left, Mike McGrevey walked by Hodges on the way out.

"Great move, Hodji," he said, grinning. "Ignore the hit and run. Make the kid look bad. He'll be gone in a week."

McGrevey slapped him on the back and moved off. Hodges, watching him leave, was no longer so sure.

In the stadium parking lot, Jenny waved to the security guard and guided the family minivan out onto the street, heading for the expressway. As she drove, she listened to Wally Holland's postgame summary on the radio.

"By all accounts, despite the loss, Heywood's debut was a rousing success," Holland was saying. "He's the talk of baseball and the toast of the town. I'm sure at this moment he's one very excited young man."

Smiling, Jenny glanced over at her son, who was seated next to her. He was sound asleep.

Facing the press was one thing; facing John "Blackout" Gatling was another. Billy got his chance the following night.

The Twins were locked up in another tough ball game with the

Tigers, and Gatling was pitching. He looked as menacing as ever, but this night his control was off. With one out in the eighth inning, he had walked two men and was about to walk a third. Dripping with sweat, he gazed in at the sign, then delivered. It was ball four, and suddenly the bases were loaded.

In the dugout, Mac shook his head. "Gatling's done. We've got to get him out of there."

"Yeah," said Billy, "let's go with Bowers."

"Right. I'll break the news to Blackout."

Billy waved him off. "That's okay, I'll do it."

"Uh, son, he doesn't like to come out of games," Mac said.

"Who does?" Billy answered, bounding up the steps. "Time, ump!"

On the bench, Mike McGrevey chuckled. "Billy versus Blackout? This should be good."

Billy strode to the mound.

When Billy reached the pitcher's mound, Blackout snapped, "What do you think you're doing here?"

"You're a little wild high. I think you're overstriding."

"Get lost, little boy," said Blackout, turning his back and rubbing the ball between his palms.

Billy's face turned pale, but he held his ground. "Uh, well, I'm going to bring in Bowers."

Blackout whirled. "No, you're not, rat boy. Not if you want to live to see puberty."

"That's enough, John," said Lou, who along with Mark Hodges had approached the mound.

"Hey, it doesn't matter to me, All-Star. Take a number. I'll kill you, too."

Lou gazed at him steadily. "I said, that's enough."

"Whose side are you on?" Blackout roared.

"His," said Hodges, stepping between Billy and the enraged

44

pitcher. "He's the manager."

As Blackout stared at Hodges, Billy took a step toward the bullpen and signaled for Bowers. But Blackout wasn't done.

"I've got news for you," he told Billy. "You don't take me out, not if you want to win."

"Why? You think Bowers can't pitch? You think you're the only relief pitcher we've got?"

"Hey, I didn't say that," Blackout replied.

"That's what it sounds like."

Jim Bowers arrived at the mound and reached out for the ball. Blackout just glared at him.

"I just want you to know," said Bowers, "I had nothing to do with this."

Blackout slammed the ball to the artificial turf. As it bounced high into the air, he stalked off the mound toward the dugout.

Later, in the clubhouse, Lou Collins looked over the postgame buffet and picked out an apple. Biting into it, he turned to Lonnie Ritter.

"You know, the kid's not doing too bad."

Lonnie nodded. "Shorty's really working out there. Boom! Takes out the big fella. Boom! Puts in Bowers."

"Boom! Loses the game," said Pat Corning.

"Yeah," Mike McGrevey added, "what do you say we let him win one before we put him in the Hall of Fame."

As McGrevey reached for a turkey sandwich, Billy walked in.

"Tough loss, guys," he said. "I really thought we were going to win that one."

"We're not going to win anything with a kid for a manager," said Spencer Hamilton.

The clubhouse went silent. Billy stood gazing at the floor. Then he looked up at Hamilton.

"It seems to me you didn't win last year with Jackson," he said.

45

"And you couldn't win this year with O'Farrell either. So maybe I'm not the problem."

He glanced around the room and mustered a smile. "Maybe the problem is, you guys forgot how much fun this is. You're major leaguers. You're on baseball cards! What could be better?"

"A multi-year deal worth big bucks, that's what," said McGrevey.

"Don't you understand?" Billy said. "You guys get to play baseball every day. You get to go to Yankee Stadium and play in the same outfield as Joe DiMaggio and Mickey Mantle. You get to go to Fenway Park and step into the same batter's box as Ted Williams. Look, don't worry about winning and losing. Just go out and play, have fun. If you make an error, forget it. If you strike out, so what? I don't care, as long as you hustle.

"Look, tomorrow's an off day. This season starts Thursday. I want everybody here early. We're going to try some things. We're going to have a little fun."

"I hate fun," said Blackout.

The players laughed. Grinning, Billy took a bunch of grapes off the table, popped one into his mouth, and walked jauntily into the manager's office. The players might have been surprised to know that when he closed the door, his hands were shaking.

9

Lots of kids go to Valley Fair Amusement Park for their birthday. Very few get to take an All-Star first baseman with them.

It was Thursday, the Twins' day off, and for Billy's twelfth birthday he had invited Chuck, Joey, Jenny, and Lou Collins to join him at Valley Fair. They rode the Ferris wheel and Joey ate junk food. They played bumper cars and Joey ate junk food. They tried a new ride called the Corkscrew and Joey ate junk food. In between, they talked and laughed . . . and Joey ate junk food.

As Billy and the others made their way through the park, they were stopped again and again to sign autographs. The amazing thing was that Billy was signing as many as Lou!

Finally Lou begged the boys for a break. While they hopped into one of the big white cars on the water ride, he stayed behind with Jenny. There was a bridge over the lake at the end of the ride, and that's where the two of them headed.

"Do you think he'll be okay?" Jenny asked him.

"Are you kidding?" Lou said, munching on a corn dog. "This is nothing compared to the Corkscrew."

Jenny smiled. "I was thinking in slightly larger terms."

"Oh, you mean like life?"

"Yeah," she said. "I mean, this whole baseball thing is so bizarre."

Lou shrugged. "Well, he is taking on an awful lot for a little kid."

"I know. I just worry so much. I'm the only one around to take care of him."

"What about you?" asked Lou.

"What *about* me?"

"Who takes care of you?"

"I do okay by myself," she said.

As they started across the bridge, Lou asked, "When was the last time you went out on a real date?"

"A real date?"

"Yeah, you know," Lou said, gesturing with his half-eaten corn dog. "You go to a restaurant with a guy you don't know very well, you sit at a table, you eat food that's not on a stick."

She looked out over the lake. "Well, let's see. Today's Thursday. So my last 'real' date would have been . . . fourteen years ago, with my husband."

"Well, at the risk of breaking a pretty impressive streak, how do you feel about going to a movie sometime?"

"What happened to food that's not on a stick?" she asked.

He grinned. "We can do that, too."

As their eyes met, Billy's voice rang out. "Mom! Mom!"

They looked up and saw Billy, Chuck, and Joey speeding toward them in the big white car. Billy called out again.

"What did he say?" Jenny asked.

Just then the car hit the lake. Water cascaded into the air, drenching Lou and Jenny.

"I think he said get off the bridge," Lou replied.

The following day they were back at the ball park again. Billy, in keeping with his promise to make the game more fun, had decided to coach at third base. He paced back and forth, calling out encouragement to his players.

The tactic seemed to working, because with two outs in the first inning, Mickey Scales hit a booming triple to right. The next batter was Pat Corning, and as he stepped into the box, Scales

48

faked a move down the third-base line toward home plate. The pitcher, clearly distracted, ran the count to three balls and no strikes.

"Time, ump," Billy called.

He trotted toward the plate and huddled with Corning.

"Take this pitch," Billy told him. "If it's ball four, I want you to try that play we worked on today."

Corning asked, "Are you sure it's legal?"

"Of course."

"I don't know," said Corning. "I mean, it sounds like a Little League play."

Billy shook his head. "No way. Ty Cobb and Wahoo Sam Crawford used to do the same thing back in the early 1900s. Just try it, okay?"

Corning shrugged. "You're the boss."

On his way back, Billy whispered to Scales, then took his position once again in the coaching box. With the next pitch, Scales bluffed toward home, but it didn't matter. The pitch was low and away, ball four.

It was called a walk, but Pat Corning wasn't walking. He lowered his head and sprinted to first. When he got there, he didn't stop. He rounded the bag and headed for second!

The catcher froze, unsure of what to do. The shortstop, also confused, finally moved to cover second base and motioned for the ball. The moment the catcher released his throw, Mickey Scales broke for the plate.

Seeing Scales, the second baseman intercepted the throw and fired it back home. But he was too late. At almost the exact same moment, Corning slid safely into second and Scales beat the return throw home.

The Twins' bench erupted, greeting Scales with grins and high fives. By the time Lou Collins stepped to the plate, the pitcher was thoroughly rattled. He threw a pitch straight down the middle of the plate and Lou belted it. The ball sailed high and deep, finally coming to rest far beyond the fence, in a remote corner of the upper deck.

From the dugout, Mac looked out at Billy and gave him the thumbs-up. Billy grinned and pumped his fist.

If the Twins had been slumbering, that inning was their wake-up call. Suddenly they were everywhere, vacuuming up grounders, chasing down fly balls, making impossible catches and pinpoint throws. They were clobbering the ball, taking the extra base, laying down the perfect bunt. And Billy was with them every step of the way, calling the plays and offering helpful advice.

They won that game, and the next, and the next. The revitalized Twins were the talk of baseball.

Billy, Chuck, and Joey spoke about it one evening as they played Monopoly at Billy's house.

"Unbelievable," said Chuck. "Six wins in a row."

Billy said, "Yeah, the best thing is I don't have to fire myself."

Joey rolled the dice and landed on Go.

Billy shook his head sadly. "Too bad. Have to go to jail."

"What do you mean?" said Joey. "When you landed on Go you got five hundred dollars."

"I know, but you're the third person. Third guy on Go always goes to jail."

Joey looked at Chuck, who nodded in confirmation.

"Oh, man," Joey said.

Then Chuck grinned and said, "You are so lame. Here's your money."

"Really?" Joey said, brightening. Then he quickly added, "I knew that."

As he counted his money, the doorbell rang. Jenny entered

from her room and moved toward the door. She was wearing a new dress and had just finished applying her makeup.

"Wow," Chuck breathed when he saw her.

Jenny blushed. "What?"

Billy said, "You look great, Mom. Um, I mean, you always do. But now you do, too."

"Thanks," she said, laughing.

She opened the door, and there stood Lou Collins.

"Hi," he said.

"Hi," she answered.

Joey and Chuck yelled, "Loooo!"

"Hey, guys, how's it going?" Lou said.

"Now, Billy," said Jenny, "you're sure you're okay with this, right?"

"I think it's great. My mom on a date."

Jenny chuckled. "Yeah, film at eleven."

She kissed Billy on the cheek, then took Lou's arm and was gone. The minute the door closed, Chuck fell into a faint on the couch.

"Ooh," he moaned. "Ooh, Lou and your mom . . ."

"Give me a break," said Billy.

Joey made kissing noises and said in a high-pitched voice, "Oh, Lou, I love you so much."

Billy said, "That's it. You're dead, both of you."

When he chased them down the hall, he didn't look like the manager of the Minnesota Twins.

10

Billy sat in the airport lounge with Mac McNally, waiting to leave on his first road trip.

"Hey, Mac," he said, "do any of our guys doctor the ball? I mean, like, throw a spitball? I don't care. I just think I should know."

"Listen, I don't teach the spitter," Mac replied. "It's a totally illegal pitch, and I'm against it. On the other hand, a little piece of sandpaper, right under the heel of your glove . . ."

As Billy listened, a shadow fell across his face. He looked up and saw Blackout Gatling towering above him. The big man shifted awkwardly from foot to foot.

"I was looking at some of the tapes. What you were saying about my mechanics was right. So, uh, I guess what I'm saying is, you're not a rat boy."

"Thanks," Billy said, relieved.

Blackout turned and moved off.

A few minutes later, Jenny Heywood and Lou Collins emerged from an airport gift shop. Jenny was holding a shopping bag.

"Here, Billy," she said, reaching inside the bag. "Toothbrush, toothpaste, and shampoo. And I want you to use them."

Billy checked to see if anyone was looking. "Okay," he said, taking them quickly.

"And Lou, remember," she went on. "I don't care if you don't get a hit the whole road trip. Just keep an eye on Billy, got it?"

"I got it, I got it."

"Mom," sighed Billy, "you've already got Mr. Goslin watching me. How many babysitters do I need?"

"Mr. Goslin is not a babysitter. He's a chaperone. Lou is a babysitter."

"This is a joke," Billy muttered.

Jenny said, "I don't suppose there's any way you could just manage home games, is there?"

Billy had been looking forward to the road trip as a great adventure. He would be out of town and on his own, seeing new people and places. The one thing he hadn't counted on was boredom.

No one had told him about the long hours away from the ball park, waiting in airports and killing time at the hotel. And no one had warned him about meals with Arthur Goslin and Mac McNally, where table talk revolved around such exciting topics as clothing bargains and investment opportunities.

Billy sat in the dining room of the team's Boston hotel, listening to Arthur drone on.

"They called the bond last month," Arthur was saying, "so I took the money and put some in munis and the rest in this flyer. It's an oil company in Colombia."

To Billy's great relief, Arthur was interrupted by the hotel manager who stood by the table fidgeting nervously.

"I'm sorry to bother you, gentlemen, but there's a disturbance with one of the players up in room four fifteen."

Arthur and Mac looked at each other. "Bowers," they said in unison.

"I apologize, sir," Arthur told the manager. "We'll handle this right away."

Seeing his chance, Billy bolted upright and scooted back his chair.

"I'll go," he said. "This is a disciplinary matter. That's the manager's job."

Before they could protest, Billy was gone. A half hour later, he still hadn't returned.

"What do you think?" asked Arthur, glancing at his watch.

Mac, who was too involved with his steak to have noticed anything, barely looked up from his plate. "I'm sure Billy's got it under control."

"Probably. Still, I don't know what could be keeping him this long."

Outside, Spencer Hamilton was just returning from an evening stroll. As he approached the hotel entrance, he noticed something streaking downward. A moment later there was a splash over to his left.

"Bite me," he said, and kept walking.

Five stories up, Billy stood at the open window of Jim Bowers's hotel room, holding a water balloon in each hand. Next to him were Bowers, Mickey Scales, and Tucker Kain.

"How did that miss?" Billy said.

"I can't stress this enough," said Bowers. "You've got to allow for the wind factor. It's vital."

Kain pointed excitedly. "Wait a minute, wait a minute. McGrevey, eleven o'clock."

Bowers shrugged. "It's too easy. His head's so big it's not even fair."

As McGrevey approached, Scales called out out to Billy, "Target in sight."

Bowers licked a finger and held it out into the breeze. "Give it three feet to the left."

Billy held another water balloon out the window and said, "Bombs away!"

Leaning out, they saw the balloon smash squarely on McGrevey's head. They ducked back inside, stifling laughter.

Behind them, someone cleared his throat. When they turned

around, they saw Arthur and Mac standing in the doorway. Billy smiled sheepishly and held out a water balloon.

"Want to try it?" he asked them.

Later, in his room, Billy picked up the phone and dialed. At the other end, a sleepy voice answered.

"Chuck?" Billy said. "Listen to this."

He picked up a card from the TV set and read off a list of movie titles.

"What's that?" Chuck mumbled.

"Movies, on the TV set right here in my room. All you do is press a button. And the great thing is, nobody knows."

Billy looked at the screen and said, "I've got to go. A new movie's just starting."

He hung up the phone and settled in, the TV remote in one hand and a slice of pizza in the other.

After all the hours of waiting at the hotel, the action had finally begun. The Twins were at Fenway Park in Boston, caught up in a tough one-run game with the Red Sox. Unfortunately, Billy was missing it. He was slumped at the end of the dugout, asleep.

Bowers turned to Mac. "And now, another exciting episode of Billy Heywood, boy narcoleptic."

"Jeez," said Mac, "and we're not even in Cleveland yet."

He reached over and shook Billy. "I thought you might want to get up for this. The Red Sox have the tying run on first."

"Huh? Sorry. What?"

Coach Cap Joseph handed him a cup of coffee. "Here you go. Maybe this'll help."

Billy took a sip and made a face. Then he took another.

"You know," he said, "it's not that bad."

There was the crack of a bat. Billy looked up in time to see the Twins turn an inning-ending double play.

He yawned. "Way to go, guys."

Sleepy manager and all, the Twins swept the Red Sox and headed for New York to meet the Yankees. At the hotel that night, Mike McGrevey sat in the lobby reading the *Wall Street Journal.* He looked up and saw Jim Bowers, Tucker Kain, and Blackout Gatling emerge from the elevator, engaged in an animated discussion.

"You see," Bowers was saying, "a pig becomes a hog at a hundred and eighty pounds."

Kain asked, "So what does that make your wife?"

"Fat," said Blackout.

McGrevey shook his head. "Don't you guys ever talk about anything that matters?"

"You mean, like money?" asked Bowers.

"I mean, like how to get off a team that's managed by a circus freak."

The elevator bell rang, and Billy stepped out.

"Well," said McGrevey, "if it isn't the bearded lady herself."

As McGrevey went back to his paper, Billy called to Lou Collins across the lobby.

"Hey, Lou, you want to get some dinner?"

"Sorry, not tonight," Lou replied. "I'm going out with some friends from college."

Billy spotted Spencer Hamilton, Lonnie Ritter, and Junior Alexander.

"How about you guys?" he said. "Want to get some dinner?"

Spencer glanced uneasily at the others. "Uh, no, I can't," he said. "I'm, uh, going out with my cousin. Right, guys?"

Lonnie nodded. "Same with me. I'm going out with my cousin, too."

Just then, three beautiful women entered the lobby. One of them waved at Junior.

"Your cousin?" Billy asked.

"Right," Junior answered.

As Billy watched the players leave, Mac came up behind him.

"Arthur and I are going to get a bite across the street. They've got a great cobbler. You want to go?"

Billy sighed. "Sure."

On their way out, they passed Jerry Johnson.

"Hey, Billy," he said, "are you any good at Sonic the Hedgehog?"

Billy explained to the puzzled Mac, "It's a video game."

"I need some help getting out of scene five," Jerry said.

"Oh, right," said Billy, "scene five's brutal."

He turned to Mac. "Look, Mac, Jerry really needs my help."

"No, sure, go ahead," Mac said. "It sounds like an emergency."

As Billy walked off with Jerry, Mac called out, "Good luck."

When Mac was gone, Billy said, "You've never played Sonic the Hedgehog, have you?"

Jerry grinned. "No, but I've eaten with Mac and Arthur."

It wasn't going well at Yankee Stadium. With two out and Mike McGrevey on the mound, the Yankees had loaded the bases. Paul O'Neill stepped to the plate.

McGrevey shook off one sign, then another. Finally he nodded and delivered. It was a hanging slider, and O'Neill crushed it.

In right field, Tucker Kain turned his back to the plate started sprinting. Glancing over his shoulder, he lunged for the ball and went crashing into the fence. He bounced off, hit the ground, and popped back to his feet. He held up his glove. Somehow he had caught the ball!

When Kain reached the dugout, the Twins mobbed him. But Mac had something else on his mind. He approached McGrevey at the water cooler.

"Hey, what happened to the scouting report? I thought we agreed not to throw him sliders."

"Guess it slipped my mind," McGrevey replied, sipping some water.

"McGrevey, you worthless prima donna, you don't deserve to wear that uniform."

"You know," said McGrevey, "you're right. I'm a disgrace to the Twins. I think you should trade me."

Mac was beside himself. He kicked at the dugout step and shouted, "As soon as we find somebody dumb enough to take you, that's just what we'll do."

"No, we won't," said Billy, who'd been listening. "We're not trading you."

McGrevey sneered. "So what are you going to do, bench me?"

"Nope. We'll play you. Every time it's your turn to pitch, you'll pitch. Nothing changes."

"I don't think that's such a good idea," said McGrevey. "I have a feeling my concentration isn't going to be that good out there. I might tend to forget some of those scouting reports."

Billy turned to walk off. "That's up to you," he said. "You're the free agent. Hey, Mac, what's the going rate for an absent-minded pitcher who can't get anybody out?"

Inspired by Kain's circus catch, the Twins rallied for five runs, highlighted by a booming homer off the bat of Lou Collins. On the mound, Mike McGrevey showed an amazing reversal of form, shutting down the Yankees and striking out the last three batters.

By the time the Twins headed home, they had swept four games from the Yankees and had moved into a tie for third place in the American League standings.

11

Billy was glad to be home, but it wasn't the same place he remembered. In this new version of home, the phone rang constantly, reporters kept coming to the door, and his room was stacked with fan mail.

Billy took it in stride, but Jenny was having a hard time getting used to it. She was reading the paper the next day when the phone rang yet another time.

"Hello?" she said. "No, I'm very flattered, but his life story isn't for sale."

The sound of the doorbell interrupted her. Setting the phone down, she took two steps toward the door and yanked it open, saying, "Please, stop—"

But it wasn't a reporter. It was Chuck and Joey. She motioned them inside and picked up the phone again.

"Look, sir, I don't care if . . . no. No. Well, then, the biography will just have to be unauthorized."

She hung up. When she turned to Chuck and Joey, she saw a third boy standing behind them.

"I don't know you," she told him.

"This is Lowell," said Chuck. "We hang around with him sometimes when Billy's not available."

Lowell nodded hello. Jenny smiled and said, "Would you guys mind taking Billy his mail?"

She motioned across the room, where several large bags bulged with letters. Each boy picked up a bag. As the phone rang again, the boys filed down the hall to Billy's room.

They found Billy sprawled on his bed, talking on the phone, with charts, graphs, and paperwork spread out before him.

Motioning his friends in, he said into the phone, "I think he's got a live arm. Yeah, I like him."

"Wedman?" asked Joey. Billy shook his head no.

Chuck glanced at his watch and said to Billy, "Hurry up."

"Uh, can I call you right back?" Billy said into the phone. "Thanks."

He hung up and asked, "What's the big rush?"

"We're late," Chuck said. "We've got the lanes reserved for one o'clock."

"One? I thought it was two."

"One, numskull. It's the only time they had."

Joey said, "Come on, we need you."

Billy shook his head. "I can't. I've got to go over this paperwork."

"Wow," Lowell said. "You sound like my dad."

Chuck glared at Lowell. "You talk when we tell you to talk."

"Hey, Thursday's an off-day," Billy said. "We've got a light workout in the morning, but then nothing. Why don't we go to Raging Waters?"

"Cool," said Lowell.

Joey whacked him with a pillow.

"Sorry," Lowell said.

Joey told Billy, "We'll meet you here Thursday, one o'clock. Deal?"

"Deal," said Billy.

On Thursday morning Billy stood on the dugout step with Mac, watching batting practice. In three swings, Jerry Johnson had managed just one ground ball to the shortstop.

"What are we going to do about Jerry?" said Mac.

"He'll be okay," Billy replied. With a dreamy look in his eye, he said, "You know, the first game I ever saw, Jerry hit a 450-foot home run to win the game."

"Son," said Mac, shaking his head sadly, "you can't afford to be a fan. It's not part of the job."

When batting practice was over, Billy turned to leave, but Mac stopped him.

"Hey, guess who I'm having lunch with today. Reggie Jackson."

Billy stared at him. "You know Reggie Jackson?"

"I was his favorite pitcher," Mac replied. "He always said he'd rather hit against me than anybody in the league. Anyway, he wants to meet you."

"He wants to meet *me*?"

"Yup. He's a big fan of yours. So what do you say. You want to go?"

"Yeah, great," Billy said with a dazed grin. "Let's go."

Mac slapped him on the back, and they started up the ramp toward the clubhouse. "I thought we'd eat at Hoolihan's," he said. "They've got a chili burger down there the size of your head."

At Billy's house a short time later, Chuck, Joey, and Lowell waited in the driveway on their bikes.

"Where is he?" said Chuck.

"I don't like this," Joey said. "We had a deal."

Chuck angrily wrenched his handlebars to one side and headed down the driveway. "Ah, forget it. Let's go. We don't need him anyway."

That afternoon, Jenny was reading when Billy burst through the door, grinning from ear to ear.

"I'm telling you, Mom," he said, "I'm bigger than Godzilla. I had lunch with Reggie Jackson, and he loves me."

"Yeah, well, good for you. You stood up your friends."

"Oh, jeez, I forgot. I better get the team to sign a couple of balls."

Jenny said, "I think you should call them and apologize."

"Yeah, you're right. I'll call them tonight."

"Good. And while we're at it, there's another thing I'm not so thrilled about. What are these movie charges?"

"Movie charges?" asked Billy, fidgeting uncomfortably.

She shot him a look. "Save it. Arthur sent me the bill. Eleven movies in three days? They must have been good."

Billy stammered, "It was Bowers. Honest. He kept making me order them. You want me to trade him? I will. I'll send him to Detroit."

"Billy . . ."

His shoulders slumped. "I'm sorry, Mom. I won't watch those movies anymore."

"Good answer," she said.

That night, Jenny entered Billy's bedroom, dressed for a date with Lou. She found her son camped out on the bed again, talking on the phone.

"Get this," Billy was saying. "He told me—what? Who told me? Reggie, who else, stupid?"

Jennie said, "Billy, I don't like that tone of voice."

He rolled his eyes and kept talking. "That was just my mom. Anyway, he said I should talk to his agent about endorsements. Huh? Commercials. Don't you know anything? He had a candy bar named after him."

Jennie gripped his shoulder. "Billy, please hang up now. I want to talk to you. Now."

He sighed and said into the phone, "Look, Chuck, I've got to go. I'll talk to you later."

Billy replaced the receiver and glared up at his mother. "Well?"

"Honey," she said, sitting down next to him on the bed, "all this notoriety is wonderful, but you have to recognize it for what it is."

"Oh, really? What is it?"

"People telling you that you're great doesn't mean it's true."

"You don't think I'm any good?" he said.

"No, no. That's not what I'm saying at all."

There was a knock at the front door, and Jenny glanced at her watch. "Oh, that must be Lou. I'm late."

She put her hand under Billy's chin and turned his face toward her.

"Look at me. You are great, but not because you can manage a baseball team. Not because famous people want to meet you. Joey and Chuck were your friends way before any of this started, and you should remember that. Billy, I don't want you to change, okay? I like you just the way you are."

"Mom, cut it out."

Billy got up from the bed and turned away, crossing his arms.

"Besides," he said in a low voice, "Lou's waiting."

12

On Friday, it was back to baseball. Billy was in the Twins' dugout, and from the press box high above the field, Wally Holland called the action.

"Jerry Johnson to the plate," he said, "trying to break out of his batting slump here in the second half of the season. He's really fighting it, though.

"All right, here's the stretch . . . and the pitch. He hits a weak ground ball, and somehow it makes it past second, into right field."

Billy leaped to his feet. "Way to go, Jerry! You see, Mac? This could be the start."

Mac watched Johnson round first base and hold on with a single.

"Son, don't you think there's something wrong when you get this worked up over a little seeing-eye grounder? Billy, we're in a pennant race. We need a batter who can help us."

Billy looked at the veteran coach, then dropped his gaze. He knew Mac was right.

After the game, Billy sat in his office, deep in thought. There was a knock at the door, and Jerry Johnson looked in.

"You want to see me?" Jerry asked.

Billy motioned him in, then leaned forward nervously. "We've, uh, decided to . . . um, well, I mean, we have to . . ."

"You have to what?"

Billy sighed. "We have to release you, Jerry. We're going to bring up Ronnie Parker from Triple A."

"What are you talking about?" said Jerry. "How can you do that to me? I thought we were friends, Billy."

"We are."

"I just need some at-bats, that's all. How am I supposed to hit if I only get to the plate once a week?" Jerry buried his head in his hands. "I can't believe this."

Billy got up and started to pace back and forth across the office. "How do you think I feel? You're my favorite ballplayer of all time. My friend Joey offered me a Wade Boggs card and a Sammy Sosa for you, and I wouldn't trade it."

"Is that supposed to make me feel better?" said Jerry. "Am I supposed to tell my wife that I just got cut by a twelve-year-old, but it's okay because he likes my baseball card?"

"I guess not," Billy said.

Jerry turned abruptly to leave. In the doorway, he looked back over his shoulder and jabbed his finger at Billy, "You're making a big mistake. I'm not through yet. I'll catch on somewhere, and when I do, I'm going to come back here and stick it in your face."

Billy watched him go. He shook his head sadly and said under his breath, "I hope you do."

That night Billy lay on his bed, gazing at his Jerry Johnson baseball card. He carefully put the card back into his collection, then got up and moved toward the living room. As he walked in, he saw his mother and Lou on the couch, kissing. Jenny looked up.

"Billy, what are you doing up?" she said, moving away from Lou and smoothing her hair.

"I don't know. I wasn't tired. Sorry I bothered you."

As Billy turned to leave, Lou said, "Are you okay? Is it Jerry?"

Billy just looked at him.

"I know it's hard," Lou said, "but it comes with the territory."

"It's not Jerry," Billy snapped. "I just wanted to watch TV."

Jenny said, "Honey, it's past your bedtime."

"So? I'm always up later than this."

"I thought we agreed," she said. "Off-nights, you have to be in bed by eleven."

Billy crossed his arms. "Okay, fine. Then Lou has to be in bed by eleven thirty. Lou, that should give you just enough time to drive home."

"Are you serious?" asked Lou.

"Yeah. If I have to have a curfew, so do you."

Jenny's eyes flashed. "You cannot give Lou a curfew."

"Yes, I can. I'm his manager."

"And I'm your mother," she said.

Lou rose from the couch and said, "Jenny, I think I'd better go. It's getting kind of late anyway."

"Ah, forget it," Billy said, turning away. "Who cares? Do whatever you want."

The next day, Billy watched Mickey Scales lay a bunt down the third base line. When the throw pulled the first baseman off the bag, Scales clearly avoided the tag but was called out anyway. Billy raced out of the dugout and confronted the umpire.

"He missed the tag!" Billy screamed. "He missed the tag!"

The umpire looked down at him. "What are you, Bob Uecker?"

"That was a lousy call. You screwed up. You were out of position."

"I saw what I saw," said the umpire. "Now go sit down."

Billy moved forward until he stood toe to toe with the umpire. "No, I'm not going to sit down, because you're a big dork!"

"Yeah, and you're a little squirt with a big mouth. Now shut up and sit down before I get mad."

Billy kicked dirt on the umpire's shoes. "Go ahead, get mad. Pop a vein, you stupid . . ."

In the stands, Jenny watched as Billy's tirade continued. At one point, the umpire's eyes opened wide, and he jerked his thumb toward the sky.

"You're gone, Heywood!" the big man shouted.

But Billy didn't leave. Kicking more dirt on the umpire, he just kept yelling. Jenny got up from her seat and hurried down toward the clubhouse.

The next day, the newspaper headline said, *Heywood Grounded! Mom Benches Billy for One Game!*

On TV, the evening news carried highlights from the press conference, where Billy appeared, dressed in T-shirt, jeans, and wraparound sunglasses.

"The way I see it," he said, "I've got to do what's best for Bill Heywood. So, for now, to avoid a more severe penalty, I will submit to my mom's suspension, but I don't agree with it. A Bill Heywood must be allowed to speak his mind to an umpire. Otherwise he can't fully do his job."

Jenny, watching the broadcast with Billy, stood up and clicked off the set.

" 'Bill Heywood'?" she asked him.

"Billy's a kid's name. Bill sounds more grown up."

Jenny said, "You're not a grownup. You're not even a teenager. And what's with this third-person nonsense?"

"What do you mean?"

"You know exactly what I mean. 'A Bill Heywood must be allowed to speak his mind.' When did all this start?"

Billy shrugged. "I don't know. That's how all the guys talk—Bo Jackson, Danny Tartabull . . ."

"Look, let Danny Tartabull's mother worry about him. I am very upset with you."

The phone rang, and Jenny reached out to answer it. Before she did, she said, "Do you remember our little talk, when you stood up Chuck and Joey? This is all part of it."

She picked up the receiver. "Hello. Oh, hi, Lou." Smiling, she settled back into the couch.

Billy left the room, muttering, "Maybe if you weren't in such a hurry to see Lou, you'd explain yourself better."

Billy was still upset two nights later, when he returned to the Metrodome. Early in the game, with Pat Corning on first, Lou Collins hit a screaming line drive that was caught by the shortstop. Corning, who had started for second, was easily thrown out. When he came back to the dugout, Billy was waiting.

"Pat, how can you get thrown out on that? The whole play was right in front of you. Where were you going?"

"I was just trying to make something happen," said Corning.

"Well, you did."

Billy turned and walked away.

Jim Bowers, seated on the bench nearby, looked up at Corning. "Is it me, or does the little fellow seem to be getting a tad edgy?"

At the water cooler, Lou approached Billy. "What you said was right, but I'm not sure about the way you said it. Pat's kind of upset."

Billy snapped, "Lou, you just play, okay? If Pat doesn't like it, let him talk to me.

"Besides," Billy added grimly, "I can't be doing that bad. We're winning, aren't we?"

13

It was just like the good old days—well, almost.

Billy, Joey, and Chuck were sitting in McDonald's. Joey was munching on McNuggets, fries, and a chocolate shake. Chuck had a Big Mac, fries, and a large Coke. And Billy? He was drinking black coffee.

"It's not my fault I never see you," he was explaining to his friends. "We're in a pennant race."

"Duh," said Chuck. "Like we didn't know."

Joey looked at Chuck, then at Billy. "Yeah, duh," he said.

"Hey, you know," said Billy, "if we win the next two against Oakland, we'll pass them. We'll be in first."

"You should start Wedman," Joey said. "He always beats the A's."

"Then why's he three and seven against the league?" Billy asked.

Chuck took a long pull on his Coke, shaking his head. "I can't believe you lost those two to the Indians. They're so lame."

"You think this is so easy?" Billy snapped. "Why don't you try it?"

"De-hype," Chuck told him. "I was just kidding around."

Joey said, "I wasn't. You should start Wedman, Billy."

"And you should leave the baseball to me. Could we just talk about something else? Please?"

Billy sipped his coffee. Joey, chewing thoughtfully on a McNugget, said, "You think, in his whole life, Batman ever ate at McDonald's or KFC?"

"Of course, he would have to," Chuck said. "Suppose Commissioner Gordon needs him and he's in a hurry, but he's really hungry. What else is he going to do?"

Joey grinned. "I'd hate to be the guy behind the Batmobile in the drive-through. You know, when Batman steps on the gas and that flame comes out . . ."

"You guys are crazy," said Billy. "The Caped Crusader does not eat fast food."

"How do you know?" Joey asked.

Chuck said, "What do you mean? Billy knows everything. He's the manager of the Twins. He's the coolest guy in the world. Just ask him."

Before the ball game that evening, Billy was interviewed for ESPN by commentator Chris Berman.

"Hello, everybody. Chris Berman for *Baseball Tonight* here in Minnesota. The fellow next to me needs no introduction. He may be a little boy, but he's a little boy with a very big job."

Billy, hands on hips, looked past Berman. "Chris, can we please get on with it?"

"Billy, I'm not going to beat around the bush. People are saying the Twins can actually win this thing. But there's a lot of baseball left. And with each game, the pressure mounts. The pundits say you're already feeling the strain, that you're cracking like a bad stucco job. How do you respond?"

"Ever since I took this job," said Billy, "everybody's been waiting for me to fail. Well, I'm not going to. I dedicated this season to my grandpa, and we're going to win it for him."

Berman said, "And yet, the stucco."

"Chris, I don't understand the question. I don't even know if it is a question."

"The feistiness of a champion," Berman chuckled into the camera. He turned to ask another question, but Billy had walked off.

Early in the game, Lou Collins walked to the plate, hoping to break out of an oh-for-eleven batting slump. He was hitting the ball hard, but it always seemed to be right at someone.

Stepping in, Lou tapped the plate and eyed the pitcher. On the first pitch, he swung. The ball shot over first base. The first baseman dove to his left and somehow snagged the ball. He scrambled to his feet and hurried to the bag, beating Lou by twenty feet.

As Lou trotted back in, Mac told him, "Tough luck, Lou. That was a good at-bat."

Billy, standing nearby, didn't say a word.

In the clubhouse after the game, Billy called Lou into his office and told him he wouldn't be playing the following night.

"You're benching me?" said Lou.

"I think you've been trying too hard."

"Why now? We're only one game out from first place."

Billy said, "Maybe if you start concentrating on baseball, you can get back in."

"Let me get this straight. You think I'm not hitting because I'm not concentrating?"

"I don't know why you're not hitting," said Billy. "That's up to you to figure out."

Just like that, the Twins started losing.

The hits that had been falling in were being caught. The long drives that had been home runs weren't clearing the fence. The miracle catches were no more, and in their place were dropped fly balls and fumbled grounders. Lou Collins watched it all from the bench, suffering with each loss.

Billy watched, too, growing more irritable by the game. When Lonnie Ritter struck out feebly at Comiskey Park, Billy jumped on him.

"Lonnie, when are you going to learn to lay off that pitch? All year, the same thing."

Wordlessly, Lonnie took a seat on the bench. Next to him, Mike McGrevey gazed at Billy and shook his head.

"And I was actually starting to like this kid."

"If he keeps ragging on me," said Blackout Gatling, "I'm going to slug the little pipsqueak. I don't care how old he is."

In the hotel room later that night, Billy flipped through the TV channels. When he didn't find anything interesting, he checked the room-service menu. Finally he sighed and picked up the phone. He dialed his mother's number, but there was no answer.

"Come on, Mom," he murmured. "Where are you?"

He hung up, then lifted the receiver and dialed again.

"Chuck, what's up?" he said.

"Oh, hi, Billy," came the voice on the other end. "Not much. Just goofing around. Nothing exciting like hanging out with major leaguers."

"Come on, I said I was sorry. Hey, maybe I can get you—"

"We don't want any more autographed baseballs," Chuck interrupted. "Listen, I've got to go. I'm sitting on Lowell."

There was a click, and once again Billy was alone.

Before the game the next day, Arthur Goslin found Billy watching batting practice high above the field, in the glassed-in Comiskey Park restaurant.

"There you are," Arthur said. "I've been looking all over the stadium for you. What's going on?"

"I just don't feel like talking to the press. Every day they keep second-guessing me. Why didn't you do this, why didn't you do that?"

"It's a compliment. They're treating you like an adult."

"Big whoop," said Billy. "You know, if they ask me one more time why Lou isn't starting . . ."

"Why isn't Lou starting?" asked Arthur.

His question still hadn't been answered later in the fifth inning, when Lonnie Ritter stepped up to the plate. The Twins were trailing the White Sox, 7-2.

Lonnie popped the ball weakly to second base. Instead of running hard to first base, he trotted partway down the line, then stopped and headed for the dugout. Billy met him there, livid.

"Why didn't you run that out?"

"I don't know," Lonnie said. "I should have. I was frustrated."

"Well," said Billy, his voice rising, "I'm frustrated with the way you've been playing. I'm fining you five hundred dollars, and if you do it again, you're suspended."

He whirled and faced the team. "And that goes for the rest of you. You guys are always talking about money and how this is a business. Well, start acting like it."

Billy sat in his office with Mac after the game. There was a knock at the door, and Lou stuck his head inside.

"You busy?" he asked Billy.

"No. You're still not playing, if that's what you're wondering."

Disregarding the comment, Lou stepped inside and closed the door behind him. "I thought you should know, Lonnie's been playing hurt. He's got two separated ribs. They took X-rays. There are no breaks, but it's painful. Most guys wouldn't even be playing. They'd be on the disabled list."

"How did it happen?" said Billy.

"Remember that collision with Cecil in Detroit?"

Billy winced and nodded.

Mac asked, "Why didn't somebody say something?"

"Lonnie made me promise," said Lou. "He didn't want to come out. He was trying to help the ball club."

Billy was still thinking about it in the bus that night, heading back to the hotel. While he was gazing out the window, Lou sat down in the seat next to him. Neither of them said a word for several minutes.

"You know," Lou said finally, "I once had a manager who said the game has to be fun, no matter what."

Billy looked up, and Lou said, "I liked playing for him."

14

Babe Ruth played it as a boy. So did Ty Cobb. It is said that when Willie Mays first started with the Giants, he would come home from the Polo Grounds and play it with the kids in his neighborhood.

The game is called stickball, and it's what you do on summer afternoons in the city if you love baseball but can't afford a bat, ball, or glove. All you need is a broomstick, an old tennis ball, a little bit of empty space between buildings, and a group of kids who dream of becoming big leaguers.

One afternoon, on a vacant lot in Chicago, a group of boys were choosing up sides to play. Phil, one of the captains, counted the players who stood around him.

"We've got one, two, three . . . oh, man, we've got nine. It's not an even number."

"If you take Sidney, we'll play you four on five," said James, the other captain.

"I don't want Sidney," said Phil. "You take Sidney."

"Forget it. Wait, I've got an idea. Let Sidney pitch for both teams."

Sidney, a small boy with blond hair, shook his head. "No way. I want to bat."

"You guys need one more?" someone asked. They turned around and saw a new boy standing there.

"Yeah," said Phil, "you want to play?"

Looking closer, Phil's eyes opened wide. "Hey, wait a minute. Aren't you Billy Heywood?"

The boy laughed. "I wish."

"Hold it, you are," James insisted.

"Everybody says that. But look, if I was Billy Heywood, what would I be doing here?"

Phil shrugged. "Yeah, I guess you're right. Okay, you can play. What's your name?"

"Bond. Jim Bond."

"All right, let's go," James said. "Bond, are you any good?"

"I'm okay."

James pointed around the lot. "Let's see, the roof's a home run, anything off the building is in play, and that trash can marks the foul line. Got it?"

The boy nodded.

Sidney pulled a pack of baseball cards from his pocket. Shuffling through them, he found a Billy Heywood card and studied it for a moment.

"Nah," he said. "Not even close."

The game started, and it turned out the new boy was right. He was okay—not great, but not too bad, either. He singled over the trash can, made a nice catch against the building, and was involved in a controversial play at third base.

But the thing they noticed most was the way he enjoyed playing. By the end of the game, the nervous frown on his face had been replaced by a wide grin.

Afterward, sweaty and tired, he stood in line for the ice cream truck with the others. Sidney slapped him on the back.

"Good game, Bond."

"Thanks," said the boy.

Sidney shook his head, chuckling. To think that he had mistaken the kid for Billy Heywood.

Jenny stood in the Minneapolis airport, waiting at the gate for the

Twins' plane to arrive. The gate door swung open, and the passengers began to file into the terminal.

Jenny waved when she saw her son. "Hi, Billy!"

He raced up and threw his arms around her.

"What's all this about?" she asked, surprised.

"I missed you, Mom."

She leaned down and kissed him. "I missed you, too."

As they drove home, Billy looked over at his mother. "It's been a weird summer, huh?"

"Yeah, I'd say a little," she said, smiling.

"I'm not handling things too well, am I?"

"Honey, you have to remember, you're just twelve years old. I mean, forget about baseball—you lost your dad, you lost your grandpa, and I'm sure there were times you were scared you were going to lose me."

"I still am," he said.

She pulled the car over to the side of the road, turned to Billy, and placed the palm of her hand against his cheek.

"Billy, listen to me very carefully. I will always be here for you. There is nothing on this earth that could ever change that . . . that could ever make me stop loving you."

Billy leaned his head against her shoulder, and she put her arm around him. It was good to be home.

In the Twins' clubhouse the following night, Lou Collins was dressing for the game when Billy came bounding through the door.

"Lou, you're starting," he said.

"Good."

Moving on to Lonnie Ritter, Billy asked, "How are the ribs?"

"I'll make it," said Lonnie, smiling.

"All right, then, let's go get 'em."

Billy wandered across the room, to where Spencer Hamilton and a few others were watching Chris Berman on ESPN.

". . . and in the American League," Berman was saying, "with one week left in the season, the only race still alive is—boy, I never thought I'd say this—for the wild card. Heywood's bunch is hanging on by a thread. The Mariners lead the Twins by four games, with four to go. So one loss by Minnesota or one win by Seattle, and the final playoff spot is determined. Hats off to the Twinkies, though. They had a fine year."

"Bite me," said Hamilton.

Billy clicked off the TV and climbed up on a chair. "Gentlemen, it's time for your favorite thing in life, a team meeting. I know you hate them, but believe me, if you think this is bad, try assembly."

Jim Bowers turned to Mike McGrevey and said, "I liked assembly."

"Figures," said McGrevey.

"Anyway, here's the deal," Billy went on. "I screwed up. I started worrying so much about winning, I forgot to have fun. And I guess I made it impossible for anybody else to have fun either. I'm sorry."

The room was silent, and then Bowers stood up. "We accept your olive branch of peace."

As Bowers sat back down, Billy said, "Now, I've got some special plays in mind. One's a pickoff play. In order for it to work, we'll have to practice it a lot. And the whole team has to help— even you, McGrevey."

Lonnie asked McGrevey, "Don't you charge extra for that?"

McGrevey stopped to think, then leaned over to Hamilton. "Hey, man, I need a comeback."

Hamilton whispered something in his ear, and McGrevey nodded. He turned to Lonnie and said, "Bite me."

Lou Collins stood up and looked around the room. "I just want to say something. Everybody's counting us out, but I've been through this before. There's one thing you've got to remember:

78

This is baseball. Anything can happen. We can still win this thing."

"You bet we can," said Billy, "and if we do, great. But win or lose, this is going to be one fun week."

15

Later that evening, Lou Collins made good on his locker-room speech. His ninth-inning home run powered the Twins to a 6-5 comeback win.

As Lou exchanged high fives with his teammates, Billy jumped up and down, as happy as any twelve-year-old fan. He became more excited when the scoreboard posted Seattle's loss.

The Twins' playoff hopes were alive for one more day.

The following morning, Billy placed a phone call to Jerry Johnson. Then he hopped onto his bike and rode out to Chuck and Joey's favorite fishing spot. He found his friends seated on a bridge, their lines dangling into the river.

"Hi, guys," said Billy, getting off his bike. They looked up at him, then turned back.

Billy sighed. "Listen, I want to be friends again. I had, like, a two-month brain cramp, but I'm better now. And I didn't bring any signed balls or bats either."

His friends didn't reply.

"Well," said Billy, "what do you think?"

Chuck said, "Maybe Lowell was right."

"What do you mean?" Billy asked.

Joey shrugged. "We were going to call you anyway. Lowell decided you were under a lot of stress, and it really wasn't your fault that you were acting that way."

"Lowell said that?"

"Yeah," said Joey. "Once we let him talk, we found out he's a pretty good guy."

Chuck asked, "Did you bring your pole?"

"I sure did," Billy said, grinning.

Billy had been right about the final week of the Twins' season. The team was having fun. Somehow, with all the pressure of the pennant race, they were playing with the enthusiasm of a Little League team.

Lonnie thrilled the crowd with his patented headfirst slides. Corning and Scales turned the double play with abandon. Blackout cranked up his scowl a notch or two, and his fastball along with it.

On the final play of the last game, Hodges lined a single to center, and Kain, who'd been at second base, raced around third and headed for home, where he arrived at the same time as the throw. In a close play, the catcher caught the ball, and Kain bowled him over. The ball popped free!

In the broadcast booth, Wally Holland exclaimed, "Who would have believed it? With a four-game sweep of the Indians, the Twins have done their part, and thus far, with three straight losses, so have the Mariners. But one more hurdle remains. A victory by Seattle tonight will still clinch the wildcard spot in the playoffs. But a loss would create a tie and force a one-game playoff. So now, the Twins can only wait and hope."

After the game, the team gathered around the clubhouse TV to watch the Mariners play the Red Sox in Seattle. The guys fidgeted and sweated and cheered as Boston carried a one-run lead into bottom of the ninth. With one out, Seattle loaded the bases, and Dave Magadan stepped to the plate.

"Mags, buddy," said Bowers, "I'm sure you're a decent human being, but die like a dog."

Lonnie covered his eyes with his hands. "Please, please, please . . ."

Lou turned to Billy and said, "What do you think?"

"I like our chances."

"Do you know something about Magadan that I don't?" asked Lou.

"No, but I'm six and one when I swallow my gum."

As the pitcher wound up, Billy took one last chew and gulped down his gum.

Magadan swung and hit a vicious ground ball. The second baseman stabbed it, flipped to short, and the shortstop fired to first for the last two outs of the game.

The Mariners had lost!

The Minnesota clubhouse erupted. Players screamed, leaped, and danced for joy. In the midst of it all, Billy glanced over at Lou.

"Told you," he said, grinning.

Much later, in the darkened stadium, Billy sat on the pitcher's mound, lost in thought. Jenny and Lou watched him from the dugout.

"Give me a second," Jenny said. She stepped onto the field and made her way to the mound.

"Hi," she said.

Billy looked up with a wistful smile. "I was just thinking about Grandpa. I bet he'd be pretty happy about all this."

"I bet he would."

She settled onto the ground next to him. For a few minutes they were silent, gazing up at the empty stands.

"Mom?" said Billy.

"Yes, dear."

"I'm tired of being a grownup."

In the pressbox, the last of the sportswriters packed up his things. A security guard made the rounds of the concession stands, locking them for the night. The box office manager shut down his computer, stretched and yawned.

On the pitcher's mound, Jenny Heywood leaned over and gathered Billy into her arms.

16

It was a sunny autumn day in the Twin Cities. Outside the Metrodome, vendors hawked T-shirts, jackets, and baseballs. A polka band wore Twins' caps and played an original tune called "The Pennant Polka." Fans streamed into the Metrodome by the thousands, among them a little girl holding a transistor radio to her ear, listening to Wally Holland's excited pregame chatter.

"This is it, ladies and gentlemen," Holland was saying. "One game to decide who goes on and who goes home."

In the manager's office, Billy sat at his desk, hunched over a math textbook and notepad, when Mac walked in.

"Doing your homework?" asked Mac.

"Yeah. School started again, you know."

"We've got a relatively big game today, kid."

Billy looked up at him. "I've got a relatively big math test. I can't have this hanging over my head."

"Math, huh?" said Mac. "I hate math. I've heard it always helps to write it down, though."

On the radio, Wally Holland continued. "You've worked all season long, and now it comes down to this. You wonder what goes through the minds of the players and coaches in pressure situations like these."

Mac went to the chalkboard and Billy read him the problem. "Okay," said Billy, "if Joe can paint a house in three hours, and Sam can paint the same house in five hours, how long does it take them to paint it together?"

"Hold on. You didn't say it was a word problem." Mac looked

around and called, "Scales, get over here."

Mickey Scales finished lacing up his shoes and approached the chalkboard.

"What's up?" he asked.

Mac said, "If I can paint a house in three hours, and you can paint it in five, how long will it take use to paint it together?"

Scales just stared at him, chewing his gum.

"Hey, Lonnie!" called Mac, seeing Ritter walk by.

Lonnie walked over, and Mac told him, "It takes me three hours to paint a house and you five. How long to do it together?"

"What color paint?" said Lonnie.

"Glad I asked," Mac muttered.

Up in the booth, Wally Holland went on, "And the question is, which team will deal with it better? I'll tell you, folks, you can cut the tension with a knife."

By now a large group had gathered around the chalkboard.

"Look," said Pat Corning, chalk in hand, "it takes eight hours. Five plus three."

Spencer Hamilton grabbed the chalk from him. "No, that's no right. There's two of them. So it only takes four hours."

"I should know this," said Larry Hilbert. "My uncle's a painter."

Blackout grunted, "Why don't they just get a house that's already painted?"

Tucker Kain took the chalk, stood motionless in front of the board, and finally said, "I don't know, man. Eight sounds good to me."

Just then, Jim Bowers approached.

"Tucker, my good man," he said. "The chalk, if you please."

He jotted a formula on the board, then wrote his answer: 1-7/8.

"Wow," said Billy, "are you sure?"

"But of course, my diminutive leader. Long have I been familiar with the exactitudes of the mathematical world."

84

Flipping the chalk to Billy, he turned and walked away. Impressed, the others watched him leave.

"Great!" Billy exclaimed. "Well, now that the pressure's off, we can just play ball."

When the team filed out onto the field, they were greeted by a roar from the crowd. Billy looked up into the stands and spotted his mother in her usual place, next to the dugout. Sitting beside her were Chuck and Joey.

Billy trotted over and gave his mom a kiss.

"Remember," said Chuck, "don't let Griffey beat you."

Joey chimed in, "Hey, Billy, you know what you should do? You should start Wedman."

"I had a feeling you'd say that," Billy replied, smiling.

The lineups were posted a short time later, and they brought a gasp from the crowd.

"Who would have thought it?" exclaimed Wally Holland. "In the biggest game of the year, Billy Heywood has given the starting assignment to little-used Bill Wedman. It's the most daring gamble of Heywood's young career, and we'll see whether it pays off."

Over the first five innings, the gamble paid off handsomely. Wedman was pitching his finest game ever, outside of Joey's dreams, and the game was scoreless. But in the sixth, Seattle put two men on base, and the always-dangerous Ken Griffey, Jr., strode to the plate.

"Well," Holland said, "Billy Heywood really pulled a rabbit out of his hat with this one. But his luck may be running out. Two on, two out, as Griffey steps in."

Billy and Mac watched from the dugout as Wedman leaned in for the sign, took a deep breath, and delivered.

"There's a long drive," Holland shouted, "way back! That one is long gone. Ladies and gentlemen, people take shorter vacations than that. So, with one flick of Ken Griffey's powerful wrists, the Mariners jump to a 3-0 lead."

As Griffey crossed the plate, the Twins' dugout was silent. In the stands nearby, Chuck turned to Joey.

"I told him. Didn't I tell him about that guy? Why doesn't anyone listen to me?"

Joey just shook his head. "It's a shame. It's just a shame."

But the Twins weren't about to give up. In the seventh, back-to-back singles put men on first and third, with light-hitting Mickey Scales coming to bat.

"I think we ought to pinch hit for Mickey," Mac told Billy.

"No way, Mac."

In the on-deck circle, Scales looked back toward the dugout. "You want me to hit?"

Billy nodded. Scales took one last practice swing and moved into the batter's box.

"Remember," Mac called to him, "be aggressive. Be a hitter."

On the first pitch, Scales stepped into the ball and sent it rocketing in a high arc toward the left field foul pole. It would reach the stands, but would it be a fair ball? The umpire, straddling the line, gazed up at the ball. He signaled home run!

Scales floated around the bases, a dazed grin on his face. When he reached the plate, he was mobbed by his teammates.

Mickey Scales had come through. The game was tied, 3-3.

It stayed that way until the ninth inning. Jim Bowers, who had replaced Wedman in the eighth, finished his warmup tosses, then watched Ken Griffey approach the plate. The Mariner superstar was 3-for-3, including two singles and his sixth inning home run.

Afraid to give him anything good to hit, Bowers walked Griffey on five pitches. Griffey, representing the go-ahead run, had excellent speed and was a definite threat to steal.

Billy watched him trot to first, then turned to the bench with an impish grin on his face.

"Fellas, remember that play we've been working? Now's the time."

Mac looked up in alarm. "Billy, this is too important a time for us to be screwing around with everybody's concentration."

"Come on, Mac, it'll be fun."

Mac stared at him, then smiled. "Oh, well. This whole season's been crazy anyway. Hey, Hodges!"

Mac flashed a series of special signals, ending up by wiggling the brim of his cap. The signals were passed around the dugout, onto the field, and into the bullpen, where Roberts, the security guard, nodded and wiggled his cap as well.

On the mound, Jim Bowers watched Griffey take his customary big lead. Bowers stepped off the rubber and fired a pickoff attempt, but Griffey easily made it back to the base.

Dusting himself off, Griffey smiled at first baseman Lou Collins. "You're wasting your time throwing after me. I'm going to steal second, I'm going to steal third, and I might just steal home."

He moved off the bag again, and this time his lead was huge. Bowers looked in for the sign, then glanced toward first. Once again he fired over there, and as Griffey dove back, Lou dove as well, trying to corral the throw. There was a cloud of dust, and Lou emerged, looking for the ball.

In the Twins' dugout, players yelled at him and pointed to a spot along the railing, up the right field line. In the bullpen, Roberts leaped from his seat to avoid the ball. Tucker Kain raced in from right field, pointing and shouting as he ran. At last, Lou noticed the activity in the bullpen and hurried up the line in belated pursuit.

In the broadcast booth, Wally Holland was going nuts. "Here comes Kain in from right. And Griffey heads for second. He may try for third!"

Meanwhile, Jim Bowers took a few quick steps off the mound and casually flipped the ball to Pat Corning at second. Griffey, dumbfounded, was out without even a slide.

"Wait a minute!" screamed Holland. "The ball never left Bowers' hand! He had it all the time! Unbelievable! Griffey is out at second, and Casey Stengel just sat up in his grave and applauded."

The Twins' dugout was a madhouse. Billy, grinning like a maniac, raced up and down the bench, exchanging high fives with everyone in sight. On the mound, Bowers bowed grandly to the crowd.

Three innings later it was a different scene. With the game still tied and Blackout Gatling on the mound, the Twins had put a man at second base with two outs. There was a hard grounder to third, and as Larry Hilbert moved in front of it, the ball hit a pebble. It took a bad hop over his shoulder, and the runner sprinted home.

The batter was thrown out at second, but the damage had been done. The Twins trailed 4-3. They were only three outs away from elimination.

17

When the players filed into the dugout, everyone was quiet—except for Billy.

"Come on, guys," he said, clapping his hands and pacing back and forth in front of the bench. "Let's get it back."

The first batter, Pat Corning, popped weakly to third and was out. As Mickey Scales moved toward the plate, Billy noticed Larry Hilbert sitting on the bench with his head down.

"Hang in there, Larry," Billy called to him.

"How could I miss that grounder?" Hilbert said. "I was right there."

Billy took a seat next to him. "You want to know something? The exact same thing happened to Freddie Lindstrom in the twelfth inning of the seventh game of the 1924 World Series."

"It did?"

"That's right," Billy said. "And you know what Lindstrom did after that? He stepped up to the plate in the bottom of the inning and ripped a game-winning double."

Billy clapped him on the shoulder. "Now grab a bat, Larry. You're on deck."

Mac watched as Hilbert strode to the bat rack with a look of determination on his face.

"Son," Mac told Billy, "I realize this ain't exactly the time, but Lindstrom never hit a double. The ball that took a bad hop ended the game."

"I know that," said Billy. "But Larry doesn't."

Mickey Scales, whose home run had tied the game in the

seventh, stepped into the box. He took a couple of tosses outside, then swung at the next pitch and hit a wicked line drive down the third base line. The Mariners' third baseman dove, his body parallel to the ground, and caught the ball. What had looked like an extra-base hit was instead the second out.

As Larry Hilbert strode purposefully to the plate, Lou came up behind Billy. "Great game, isn't it."

Billy nodded, then said, "Hey, you're up next. Why aren't you on deck?"

"Have you seen your mother?" Lou asked.

"She's right behind the dugout. Why?"

"I just asked her to marry me."

Billy stared at him. "What did she say?" he asked finally.

"She said to ask you."

There was a roar from the crowd as Larry Hilbert rapped a sharp single to left. He sprinted to first base, pumping his fist. The Metrodome was in an uproar.

Billy turned to Lou. "Hit a homer."

"What?"

"Hit a homer and I say it's okay."

Lou got his bat from the bat rack and headed for the plate.

"Hey, Lou!" Billy called after him. "You can marry her even if you don't."

Lou grinned. "Thanks."

"And Lou?"

"Yeah?"

"Watch for the slider, low and away."

High above the field, Wally Holland leaned into the microphone. "It's all up to Lou Collins. And Twins fans, tell me, who would you rather have up there?"

Lou stepped in. The crowd was on its feet. The Twins, rally caps on, lined the top step of the dugout, yelling encouragement to

Lou. Billy stood with them, watching the scene unfold, a smile on his face.

"So it's Randy Johnson," continued Holland, "making a rare relief appearance for the Mariners. But in a situation like this, manager Lou Piniella's pulling out all the stops. Six foot ten, with a nasty slider, Johnson's been almost unhittable over the last few weeks. Lou taking his time. All right, here's the pitch . . ."

There was a loud crack.

"Oh, my," yelled Holland, "there's a long drive. It could be, it might be . . ."

The crowd screamed, imploring the ball to reach the stands. Billy and Mac used every ounce of body English, trying to boost it over the fence.

And suddenly, out of nowhere, Ken Griffey reached up and snared the ball.

Wally Holland sighed. "Oh, my."

Lou Collins, almost to second base, stared out at the wall. Then he took off his batting helmet and let it drop to the ground.

The Mariners, meanwhile, raced for the mound and piled on top of Johnson. They were going to the playoffs. The Twins weren't.

Billy met Lou halfway to the dugout.

"You did great, Lou," he said.

"Thanks."

Later, in the clubhouse, the Twins milled about, still in a state of shock, not wanting the season to end.

"Hey," yelled Lonnie Ritter, "it was still a great year."

"Most fun I've ever had," said Corning.

"I don't know," said Bowers. "I kind of miss O'Farrell."

The door to the manager's office opened, and Mac and Billy came out. Behind them were Arthur Goslin, Jerry Johnson, and Lou Collins.

"Can I have everybody's attention?" said Mac. "The manager has something to say."

Billy stepped forward and looked around the room.

"You know," he said, "the Brooklyn Dodgers had a saying: Wait till next year."

"Yeah," Spencer Hamilton yelled, "because next year we'll win it all!"

As the team shouted its approval, Scales asked Lonnie, "The Dodgers played in Brooklyn?"

Billy held up his hand. "I really think we can do it. The thing is, though, we're making a little change. I'm retiring. Between fishing and Little League, I just don't think I can do the job."

The room fell silent.

"You can't step down," said McGrevey. "I just signed a new contract."

"Well, if you want out . . ."

"Nah, that's okay. The only advantage to being on another team is getting to pitch to these jokers."

Billy went on, "Mac's taking over for me, and Jerry's rejoining us as third base coach and hitting instructor."

Bowers shook his head, stunned. "This can't be. You're the only manager I ever had who grasped the intricacies of the water balloon."

"Billy," said Blackout, trying his best to look menacing, "you can't leave."

"It's not like I'm going anywhere," Billy said. "I'm still the owner. And the way I figure it, if I struggle in junior high, I can always come back."

As he spoke, Roberts, the security guard, entered the clubhouse.

"Excuse me, Mr. Haywood," he said. "But, they're still here."

"Who?" asked Billy.

"Everybody."

The players moved up the ramp and into the dugout, where they looked in amazement at the stands. The crowd hadn't left. They were on their feet, cheering and calling for the team.

Lou stepped out onto the field, and there was a roar. "Lou! Lou! Lou!" shouted the fans.

Lou tipped his cap, then moved toward the stands and helped Jenny over the railing. She joined him on the field, and he gave her a big kiss. The crowd loved it.

"We want Billy!" someone called.

The chant began, "Bil-ly! Bil-ly! Bil-ly! Bil-ly!"

It spread around the stadium, and fans craned their necks, looking for the Twins' manager.

Billy came out of the dugout a moment later, and the crowd yelled their approval. Looking up into the crowd, he smiled and waved. He spotted Chuck and Joey, who were busy telling everyone around them that Billy Heywood was their best friend.

Billy joined Jenny and Lou, then stepped back and let the sights and sounds wash over him.

"You know," he said to Lou a few moments later, "this is a great ending for my essay."

"What essay?"

"I've got a paper due Friday," said Billy. "'What I Did on My Summer Vacation.'"

About the Author

Ronald Kidd is the author of *Sammy Carducci's Guide to Women, Sizzle & Splat, Second Fiddle,* and other books for children and young adults. A producer of children's books and records, his honors include the Children's Choice Award, a Grammy Award nomination, three gold records, and a nomination for the Edgar Allan Poe Award. He lives with his wife in Nashville, Tennessee, where on summer evenings he can be found at the ball game, eating peanuts and Cracker Jack.